THE JIGSAW PUZZLE KING

THE JIGSAW PUZZLE KING

GINA MCMURCHY-BARBER

DUNDURN
TORONTO

Publisher: Scott Fraser | Acquiring editor: Kathryn Lane | Editor: Susan Fitzgerald
Cover designer: Laura Boyle
Cover image: shutterstock.com/Olga_Angelloz
Printer: Webcom, a division of Marquis Book Printing Inc.

Library and Archives Canada Cataloguing in Publication

Title: The jigsaw puzzle king / Gina McMurchy-Barber.
Names: McMurchy-Barber, Gina, author.
Identifiers: Canadiana (print) 20190165154 | Canadiana (ebook) 20190165162 | ISBN
    9781459746060 (softcover) | ISBN 9781459746077 (PDF) | ISBN 9781459746084 (EPUB)
Classification: LCC PS8625.M86 J54 2020 | DDC jC813/.6—dc23

We acknowledge the support of the Canada Council for the Arts and the Ontario Arts Council for our publishing program. We also acknowledge the financial support of the Government of Ontario, through the Ontario Book Publishing Tax Credit and Ontario Creates, and the Government of Canada.

Care has been taken to trace the ownership of copyright material used in this book. The author and the publisher welcome any information enabling them to rectify any references or credits in subsequent editions.

The publisher is not responsible for websites or their content unless they are owned by the publisher.

Printed and bound in Canada.

VISIT US AT

⌖ dundurn.com | 🐦 @dundurnpress | ⎔ dundurnpress | 📷 dundurnpress

Dundurn
3 Church Street, Suite 500
Toronto, Ontario, Canada
M5E 1M2

For Dave, Nathan and Kristen, Cameron, Archie,
and Dexter

"My cup runneth over."

CHAPTER 1

"How's it going, Warren?" asked Mom, that first day in our new house.

"I'm bored," I said, picking at the scab on my knuckles. I got the scratch the day we left the old farmhouse in Smiths Falls when I was trying to make Jelly, my cat, go into her kitty kennel. Looking at the orange furball now curled comfortably on my bed, I figured I'd been forgiven, because she looked as if she didn't have a care in the world. Life was like that for cats — simple. As long as they had their people, a bowl full of food, and a place to sleep, that was enough. "I wish I had a friend to play with."

"Now that you're unpacked, why don't you go outside and play with your brother?"

"Aw, Mom. All he wants to do is play make-believe. I need a friend who likes to do the same things I like. Bennie can barely kick a soccer ball — and forget about hockey."

Mom smiled. "Well, maybe he'll grow into those things one day. But as for make-believe, he's outside with a bunch of kids right now and they sound like they're having loads of fun playing one of his games."

"He is?"

"Uh-huh."

"Mom," I sighed, "you let him out alone? You should've told me."

"Well, I'm telling you now. Besides, he's not far." She was almost laughing at me. "So what are you waiting for?"

Outside, I followed the sounds of laughter and screams coming from the empty lot two houses over. There was Bennie, moaning and staggering after some boys and girls who darted in and around him, laughing hysterically. They urged him to catch them, but they were much too quick. My guts twisted into a knot as I watched my plan for a carefully crafted fresh start melt away in the late August sunshine. Sometimes people who didn't know Bennie thought he was weird. I liked to ease him into new situations slowly so we might avoid that.

Just then, Bennie saw me.

"Hey, everybody, that's my big brother, Wart. Can he play, too?" Blood rushed to my cheeks when some kids snickered at my dreaded nickname. I wished I had arms like Plastic Man so I could reach out and whack him for that. Instead I pretended I didn't hear him and tried to sneak away. Of course, Bennie had a different plan, and before I had time to leave he wagged his chubby arms at me and shouted, "C'mon, Wart, it's all right. You can play, too. Don't be afraid. These guys are nice."

Shoot. I was stuck. "Ha. I'm not afraid," I said as I shuffled over to the group, pretending not to notice all the stares.

"We're playin' *The Walking Dead*, and I'm the zombie," Bennie said. That explained all the moaning and staggering. "If I tag you, you'll be a zombie like me." He started up his act again, and the kids scattered in different directions, screaming. When he staggered toward me, I darted past him and joined the others running and hiding behind shrubs.

Bennie chased us as quickly as his flat feet could carry him. I knew he would be a lonely zombie if I didn't help him. It had always been like that, ever since I could remember: me helping him and keeping him from getting hurt. I was just about to step out and let him tag me when someone tapped my shoulder.

"Quick, hide behind here," said a girl, who ran behind some trees. I followed her and found some other kids were hiding there, too.

"Hi, Wart. I'm Maya. This is my brother, Taylor, and that's Luke," the girl whispered.

I picked at the bark on the tree and tried to act casual. "Actually, my name's Warren. Only Bennie calls me that."

"Well, that's a relief. It'd be seriously unfortunate if that was your real name," said Maya, giggling. The two boys sniggered.

"Bennie's funny. Does he always call you that?" asked Taylor. My stomach muscles tightened and my mouth suddenly felt parched.

"He's not supposed to call me that in public, but he forgets. It started when we were little." Just then Bennie stomped past our hiding place and moaned some more. Again Taylor and Luke laughed like it was the funniest thing on earth, and again it felt like someone was squeezing my gut.

"What grade are you in?" Maya asked, taking no notice of them.

"Six."

"Oh yeah? Me, too. Going to Rosemary Brown Elementary?"

I nodded just as the zombie tripped and fell. I heard him whimper in pain. I would have gone to help him, but Maya grabbed my arm. "Wait for a second," she whispered. "There, you see, he's all right. He's getting up now. Sometimes little brothers just have to learn to manage on their own." Maya laughed lightly as Bennie got up and stumbled after some kids, who darted around him like sparrows. "How old is Bennie?"

"Eleven," I said, peeking through the branches. I hoped he'd catch at least one kid and turn him into a zombie.

"Eleven?" Maya looked confused. "Well, then, how old are you?"

"Eleven." I glanced over at Taylor and Luke. They looked baffled, too.

"But he said you were his big brother," said Maya, now looking suspicious.

"Technically, I am his big brother … by four minutes."

"No way!" declared Taylor. "Twins? That can't be true. He's so small and so weird —"

"No, no, no. You mean different," Maya corrected. I shrugged, hoping they would let it drop. And they did, but it was an awkward silence. Finally, Maya said, "Well, he's a neat kid, and look, he's doing great."

"Right. He hasn't even tagged anyone," I said. "I should go and help him."

"Aww, he's doing fine. And he sure looks like he's having fun. So is everyone else." She was right. Bennie did look happy.

"He sure has that creepy zombie act down pat," said Taylor. "Hey, he should be a zombie for Halloween!" *Ouch.* And then it came, the question someone always asked. "So anyway, what's your brother got?" Instantly my upper lip felt prickly from beads of sweat.

Maya swatted her brother on the arm. "Shut up, Taylor," she said. "Sorry, Warren."

Taylor sneered at her. "What? I'm just asking —"

"Never mind." Maya cut him off.

"You're not my mother, Maya. I just want to know what's wrong with the kid."

I tried to laugh it off and change the subject. "Wrong with Bennie? Well, for starters, he takes my stuff without asking. And calls me Wart in public, which is pretty embarrassing. And —"

"No, not like that," Taylor blurted. "His face is weird and he acts different. Is he a retardo or something?"

Maya gasped and her cheeks turned beet red. "Just ignore him, Warren. That's what I do." She glared at him. "Sometimes I even pretend I don't have a brother."

It was too late, though. The question hung in the muggy summer air like the smell of dog poop stuck to someone's shoe. Before I could say anything, Bennie staggered across the field trying to tag some kid who was running circles around him and laughing.

"Bennie, you run like a duck," the boy teased. "Quack, quack, quack!"

That's when I snapped. "It's called Down syndrome, and yeah, maybe he's slow, but he isn't stupid! Not like some people, Taylor." I stepped out from the trees and shouted, "Bennie, come on. It's time to go. Mom needs our help with the unpacking."

Bennie stopped running and let out a sigh of relief. "Good, 'cause I'm pooped."

As we walked back to the house, I heard whispers and giggles. My fists clenched. Then someone yelled out, "See ya, Bennie. Bye, Wart."

When we got to the end of our driveway, Bennie turned back and shouted, "See you guys later! And you better watch out, 'cause next time I'm gonna catch ya and eat your brains. You'll see." Then he chuckled and waved goodbye.

CHAPTER 2

When Mom called me for breakfast on the first day of school, I had to drag myself from bed. The first day of anything new was always the worst. I'd spent most of the night worrying about what my school was going to be like and if I would make any friends. And, yes, I thought about how well Bennie would fit in.

I tried on five different shirts before I finally decided on my lucky Toronto Maple Leafs hockey jersey. Then came the hair. I tried ramming the brush through it to flatten my wiry curls, but it just turned to fuzz instead. I finally managed to tame it with a scoop of Mom's hair gel.

I walked into the kitchen. Bennie was hunched over his bowl of cereal.

"Bennie, you need to sit up, and please stop slurping," Mom said. Bennie sat up but couldn't bring the spoon from the bowl to his mouth without spilling. Mom let out a long sigh. "Well, you're not changing again. That's already the third shirt you've dirtied this morning."

When I sat down at the table, Bennie looked up and smiled. He had a milk moustache and a snotty nose.

"Mornin' Wart," Bennie mumbled as he chewed. Shredded Wheat sloshed down his chin.

"Bennie!" I groaned, pointing to his face. "Use your napkin." He wiped his face with his sleeve instead.

"You 'cited about school, Wart? I am! Gonna meet some new kids today. Aren't I, Mom?"

She smiled. "That's right, Bennie. You're going to make lots of new friends." Then she turned to me. "I see you've been into my gel again. Going for the Count Dracula look, are you?"

"Really? Does it look bad? 'Cause if it looks bad …"

"No, Warren, it's not that bad. And I hope you haven't been stressing all night. Everything's going to be fine, okay? And for the record, you always look good in that shirt."

"Ya sure do, Wart. Ya look handsome as the dickens." Bennie beamed at me, peanut butter now added to the milk and snot on his face.

"You, mister, need to wash your face and brush your hair before we leave. Then you'll be as handsome as your brother," said Mom. Bennie jumped off the chair and took off for the bathroom. "Warren, you need to eat up quick. We've got to leave for school soon."

"Mom, I'm in grade six now. I want to go to school on my own."

Mom stopped writing out her to-do list and looked up at me. "It's much better if we all go together. That way you can walk Bennie to his new classroom."

"No," I said, probably a little too loudly. "I want to ride my bike. I want to go on my own."

I could tell by the look on her face she was both surprised and disappointed. "Where's all this coming from, Warren?"

"I don't know. I just think it's time I did some stuff on my own."

"On your own? Well, I need you to help me with Bennie."

"Help you with Bennie? My whole life I've helped you with Bennie. I go with him to his physiotherapy, his speech therapy, and you even make me go to the dentist with him," I said.

Mom looked hurt. "But that's because he always feels safer when you're there."

"No, Mom. You feel safer when I'm there. Bennie couldn't care less. And it's not just appointments. If he goes to the park, I have to go. If he's invited to a friend's birthday party, I have to go, too, and you know how much I hate that. Just because we share the same birthday, does it mean we have to do everything together?"

"You were the one who always wanted it that way," said Mom.

"Yeah, when I was little! Now I'm eleven. It's time I did stuff on my own."

Mom let out a heavy sigh. "Well, you sure picked an odd time to tell me this. Anything else you want to tell me?"

"Yeah. I don't like it that Bennie and I have to go to the same school. I liked it better before where he had his school and I had mine."

Mom flung her pad of paper in the air. "Warren! I can't believe you just said that. You know what we've gone through to find a school that would give your brother the same opportunities as every other child, to treat him like they treat you." She started ramming her things into her bag. "You … you have everything and you can do everything. So why can't you see how good this is for Bennie?"

Her words cut deep and I felt like I'd shrunk. "I'm sorry, Mom. I didn't mean to upset you. But try and see things my way. It's hard enough having to go to a new school. All I want is to be my own person, and not Bennie's bodyguard or babysitter or twin brother. I just want to be my own self, and be responsible for myself, like everyone else."

Mom's annoyed look melted and she calmly picked up her pad of paper. After a long silence she said, "Fine, you can go to school on your own. But Warren, one day you'll realize that none of us is like anyone else. Bennie is your brother and nothing will change that. And I'm sorry, but we count on you to be there for him, to look out for him. Understand?"

I nodded, then wolfed down the rest of my toast, gulped my milk, and bolted out of the kitchen before she changed her mind or other objects started flying across the room.

Soon I was riding my bike toward Rosemary Brown Elementary and enjoying my freedom. I parked my bike and joined the rest of the kids heading for the school entrance. There was a lot of excitement in the air. It made me excited, too — and nervous.

A group of boys sat on the front steps, laughing and joking around. They acted like they owned the place and everyone knew it. I pictured all my old friends sitting around like that on the first morning of the new school year and wondered if they missed me as much as I missed them. I squeezed past the boys to reach the front door. Just as I pulled it open, I heard one say, "Hey, guys, take a look at the goof with the teddy bear." The rest of them sniggered. I looked back, dreading what I'd see — and sure enough, it was Bennie. *Geez!* Why did Mom let him bring his ratty old Binkie Bear to school?

"Hi, Wart," Bennie yelled at me, waving his bear happily. "Wait up."

Ignoring him, I ducked into the school and hurried toward room 5. My heart was beating like a drum roll and I was out of breath. I felt a little bad for ditching my brother, but at the same time I hoped no one knew he was calling to me.

A short-haired lady with thick-rimmed glasses stood outside the classroom. "Hello. I'm Mrs. Chapman. And you must be Warren Osborne," she said. "Come on in and find the desk with your name on it. We'll get started as soon as all the others arrive."

I wandered around until I found my desk. A moment after I sat down, I felt a tap on my shoulder.

"Hi."

I looked up to see Maya, the girl from the other day. "Hi," I mumbled, shrinking into my seat. I hoped her desk was on the other side of the room, but no luck. She dropped into the one across the aisle from mine.

"Hey, that's cool we're in the same class," she said. I nodded. "I saw Bennie down the hall. He's got Miss Jones for a teacher. She's got other kids with learning disabilities in her class. I heard that she's the best."

"Oh yeah? That's good." I turned away, pretending to be interested in the world map on the opposite wall.

Soon there was a buzz in the room as the seats began to fill. When Mrs. Chapman finally shut the door and came to the front of the room, there was still one empty desk, the one to my right. The nametag on it read *Owen B.*

"Good morning, everyone, and welcome to grade six," said the teacher. "I hope you all had a pleasant summer. Most of you have been students here at Rosemary Brown for many years, but we have a new student with us this year." My armpits were suddenly sweaty. "Why don't you stand up, dear, and tell us something about yourself?"

On cue, all the kids in the room turned to gawk at me.

As I stood, my foot caught on the desk leg and I tripped. That set off a few giggles around the room. Weak in the knees, I mumbled, "Hi, I'm Warren Osborne. I'm eleven years old. I moved here from Smiths Falls, Ontario. The population there is under nine thousand people. So that makes it a town, not a city." I turned to sit back down.

"Oh, we need a little more than that. Why don't you tell us about your family or the things you like to do?" said Mrs. Chapman.

My cheeks were on fire, and there was an annoying frog in my throat that I kept trying to clear. "Ah, well, I have a mom and a dad and a brother and a cat named Jelly. I like to play soccer, I collect hockey cards, and um, that's about it, I guess."

"And is your brother here at Rosemary Brown, too?"

I nodded.

"Bennie's really neat, and he likes to invent games, like *The Walking Dead,*" came Maya's cheerful voice beside me.

"Oh, that's nice. Which class is he in, Warren?" asked my teacher.

I shrugged.

"He's got Miss Jones," Maya said, beaming.

Everyone seemed to know what that meant, and they looked at me with new interest. My face was probably red as beets, but I still managed to meet each pair of eyes looking up at me. Maya smiled, but I gave her the stink eye and willed her to keep her big mouth shut from now on.

I was glad it was only half a day of school. When class finally let out for lunch, I hurried off to get my bike. Unfortunately, I wasn't quick enough. Maya caught up with me at the front entrance of the school.

"You're kind of sensitive about Bennie, aren't you?" said Maya.

"Yeah, maybe I am. I don't like it when people ask me embarrassing questions about him."

Maya blushed. "If this is about what Taylor said, he just doesn't know any better. He didn't mean anything by it."

"Sure, but you try hearing that stuff over and over your whole life and see how you like it." I had my eye on the door. "Anyways, never mind. He's not the first, and he won't be the last." I suddenly felt bad when I noticed Maya's cheeks shone red. "Look, I'm sorry I came off edgy, okay? I've got to go now. See you tomorrow."

I pushed open the front doors to find the same gang of boys parked on the steps. Had they even gone to class? To avoid squeezing by again, I jumped the rail and slid to the ground.

"Hey, kid, you've got a lot of nerve walking around our school looking like that," said one of them. I had no reason to think he was talking to me, so I kept walking toward my bike.

"You, kid in the Maple Leafs jersey. Didn't you hear me?" shouted the boy. I looked back over my shoulder. "Yeah, you. This here is a Vancouver Canucks school, so lose the shirt."

"Danny, the Leafs are a pretty good team," said one of the other boys. "Got some good players, like John Tavares."

"You would say something like that, Jesse. Traitor!" Danny jumped on his friend and locked his arms around his head. As they wrestled, I headed for my bike.

"I like the Maple Leafs, too," came another voice suddenly. We all turned. There was Maya standing at the top of the stairs. *Geez!* That girl was like gum stuck to my shoe.

"You would," said Danny. "You're a girl!"

"They're a good team," she said defiantly. "My dad says so."

The boys laughed and mimicked her. "My dad says so. My dad says so. Haha!"

"Mind your own business, Maya," warned Danny. Then he turned to me, his eyes narrowed. "Like I said, Canucks rule at this school. Got it?"

"Just ignore him, Warren." Maya glared right back at Danny. "I hope I don't need to tell your parents you've been bullying again." Danny's face went red as peppers. Maya stepped past the boys and walked over to me. "I'll ride home with you."

That did it. The guys started laughing, blowing kisses, and making smooching sounds.

I couldn't decide what was worse: being harassed about my favourite shirt by the school tyrant or having Maya think I needed her to defend me. Instead of trying to figure it out, I jumped on my bike and pedalled away so fast that soon my legs burned and I was gasping for air. When I reached home, I glanced down the street. No one was there except a tomcat crossing the road. Relieved, I parked my bike in the garage and went into the house.

"How come you didn't say hi to me, Wart?" Bennie asked at lunch. "I called to you at school."

I wasn't a very good liar — especially to Bennie. So I stuck my head in the fridge, pretending to look for something to eat. "You did? Never heard you. Must have been too much noise."

"Did you have a good morning?" Mom asked as she put grilled cheese sandwiches and pickles on the table. Bennie snatched up a huge handful of sliced pickles and a sandwich. "Bennie, put some of those back. Warren wants some, too."

I looked at his hands. "Not after his dirty mitts have been all over them."

"Fine, but I'm not slicing up any more," Mom said. Bennie happily stuffed his grilled cheese sandwich with the pickles and started munching. "Well, tell us about your first day."

When I was little I used to love the first day of school — meeting my teacher, seeing who was in my class, finding out what we were going to learn. Things were easier back then. "It was okay, I guess. Not much to tell."

"I got a new teacher. What's her name again, Mom?"

"Miss Jones."

"Yeah. Her name is Miss Jones. She's pretty. And I got a lot of new friends, too," Bennie said, his cheeks bulging with sandwich and pickles. "Mom, can I put some peanut butter on my grilled cheese?"

"Ugh! Bennie, why do you have to talk when your mouth is full? It's gross looking at mashed-up food oozing out your gob hole," I said.

Mom frowned at me. "Warren, you could say that more kindly. Your brother is learning and needs our patience." She turned to Bennie. "Bennie, honey, please wait until you've finished chewing the food in your mouth before talking. Remember?"

Bennie swallowed hard and bent his head low. "Sorry, Wart. Sorry, Mom. I forgot."

I felt a stab in my heart. "I'm sorry, too."

"Well, it sounds like Warren doesn't have anything to share, so why don't you tell us more about your morning?" said Mom.

Bennie beamed. "Teacher says we're gonna get a class pet — a bunny. And she says I'm gonna learn more 'bout numbers. I get to draw pictures and sing songs, too. And I got a lady who helps me. What's her name again, Mom?"

"Emma."

"Right, Emma. She's gonna help me learn to read. That's the best part." Bennie shoved more sandwich into his mouth.

"Yes, and I heard they get some of the grade sixes and sevens to volunteer to help in Miss Jones's class. Maybe that's something you could do, Warren," Mom chirped.

I pictured Danny and the other boys and wondered if any of them would sign up to help the kids with special needs. "Maybe. We'll see," I said. I couldn't help noticing how the smile quickly melted from her face.

After lunch I slipped out to the backyard to kick the soccer ball around. I bounced it off the side of my foot and then popped it up for an overhead kick. I repeated the drill until I'd worked up a sweat. I used to play soccer with Michael Jeffers back in

Smiths Falls. He was my best friend from the time I was seven. Moving was hard, but life without a best friend was the worst.

While I knocked the ball around, I heard voices and splashing coming from the yard behind our house. We hadn't met many people in the neighbourhood yet, but this was one family I wouldn't mind getting to know. They had a swimming pool.

"Good. Now do it again," said a lady's voice from over the fence. There was more splashing and someone grunting, like he was working extra hard. "You see! I knew you could do it. You're getting stronger every day. Okay, time for lunch." Then came the sound of more splashing and grunting. "That's enough for today, Owen. Up onto the deck. Wait here a minute and I'll get you a towel."

Owen? The empty desk next to mine at school belonged to an Owen. I wondered if this was the same kid from my class. If it was, why wasn't he in school today? I snuck past our hedge and tried peeking through the cracks in the fence boards but couldn't see anything.

"What ya lookin' at, Wart?" Bennie hollered from behind. I jumped out of the hedge, my cheeks burning. I hoped Owen hadn't heard.

"Who's over there?" Bennie asked.

"It's nothing. I'm just getting my ball," I said, trying to sound casual and hoping he'd let it go for once.

"No. You were lookin' at somethin' through the fence. I saw you." I tried to shush him, but he wasn't having anything to do with it. "Let me have a look, too."

Why did he have to be such a loudmouth? A small explosion went off in my brain and before I could stop myself I blurted, "Bennie, you're such a pain. Go bug someone else for once."

As soon as the words were out of my mouth, his shoulders drooped. *Crap.* I stormed out of the yard, grabbed my bike, and raced off up the street.

An hour later I snuck into the house through the back door. I heard music coming from Bennie's bedroom. I went into my own room and found Jelly fast asleep on my bed. Scooping her up in my arms, I buried my face in her furry body. I couldn't remember a time when I felt so lonely. My old life in Smiths Falls seemed so easy now, and so far away.

"I'm home." Dad was home from work early. A nanosecond later I heard Bennie thumping down the hall. I knew he would fly into Dad's arms and squeeze him like he'd been away for years.

A few minutes later, Dad popped his head into my room. "Come on, sport, we're going out for pizza," he said. "Hey, why the long face?"

I didn't feel like trying to explain. I yawned and said, "Just a little tired, I guess."

"Your mom is, too. Moving is hard work. That's why we're going out for a drive and then dinner. Get cleaned up. We're leaving in ten minutes."

When I crawled into the back seat of the car, Bennie was beaming. "Hey, Wart, we get to go out for pizza and it's not even Friday night. Aren't we lucky?"

"We could stay home instead and have one of your peanut butter and pickle concoctions," Dad joked.

Bennie gasped. "You just gave me a good idea. I'm gonna order a peanut butter and pickle pizza." He licked his lips and sighed happily.

"Try and say that five times fast," said Mom. "Peanut butter and pickle pizza."

Bennie tried and got all tongue-tied.

Soon we were all giggling and snorting. As hard as I tried, I couldn't stop imagining the look on the waiter's face if Bennie actually ordered a peanut butter and pickle pizza. My ribs hurt and my mouth was tired from smiling. And for the first time in a long while, everything seemed normal. It felt good. Real good.

CHAPTER 3

Friday morning I was in the garage breaking down some of our moving boxes before school when the TV cable guy arrived. I watched him making repairs and checking the signal in the garage. Bennie shouted at me from the top of the stairs every few minutes.

"Wart, is he done yet? Does he know it's time for *Science Nerds*? Does he know? Does he know?"

"Sounds like somebody's got a favourite show to watch." The cable man chuckled. "Everything is looking fine now. I'll just check out your TV reception and see if we've got that problem fixed." I led him to the TV room, where Bennie was already sitting cross-legged on the floor. *Science Nerds* was just starting.

"Hey, little buddy, can I just check your TV's reception? Want to make sure everything is looking good." Bennie was sitting so close to the TV he didn't hear the man. "Pretty focused, eh?"

"Yeah. When Bennie gets into his TV shows it's kind of hard to get his attention," I replied. Just then the show broke for a commercial and Bennie turned and smiled. When he saw the cable guy, he jumped up, ran over, and gave him one of his famous bear hugs.

"Thanks, mister. You saved my life." The man stood stiff, like a cardboard cut-out, then unwrapped Bennie's arms and backed away. Some people liked that Bennie was really friendly — like an excited puppy that's all over you when you first walk into a room. But some people didn't. It wasn't hard to tell what type the cable guy was.

"Ah, no problem, kid." He used the remote to check the other channels. "Okay, everything's looking good. So I'll be on my way."

"You should stay, Mr. Cable Man. The show is about Egyptian mummies. They're like zombies, you know, only they got no brains. That's 'cause their brains got sucked out the nose after they died."

As if he wanted to avoid eye contact with Bennie, the man looked over at me. "He sure is an excited little guy. Too bad I'm so busy I can't stay and watch. Well, you enjoy your show now. Bye."

As the man drove away Bennie waved from the window like they were best friends. "He sure is nice, isn't he, Wart?" Fortunately, the show came back on and I didn't have to answer. Bennie eagerly parked himself in front of the TV to learn more about how dead Egyptian mummies lost their brains.

* * *

As I rode to school later that morning, I wondered if Owen would be in class that day. He wasn't, but it seemed like I was the only one who even noticed.

"I brought my hockey card collection today. Want to see them at recess?" asked Maya.

"Sure."

"Hey, I told my dad how Danny was bugging you about your Maple Leafs jersey. He said I should tell him if Danny bugs you again. He'll call Danny's parents and have a talk."

I nearly growled. Who did she think she was? I didn't need her — or her dad — sticking up for me. "Maya, it was no big deal, and besides, I'm not afraid of Danny, or Jeff or Cam or any of those other guys, either."

The smile vanished from her face like air from a popped balloon. To change the subject, I looked over at the desk next to me. "What do you think happened to this kid?"

"Owen Bradshaw?" Maya's eyes opened wide. "I forgot, you don't know about him. He lives right behind you."

So it was the same kid I'd heard working out in the pool a few days before.

"At the start of summer holidays he had a pretty bad accident. Really, really bad."

Mrs. Chapman called for everyone's attention.

Maya leaned in and whispered, "I'll tell you about him at recess."

Over the next hour I had a hard time keeping focused on Mrs. Chapman's boring grammar lesson on homonyms, homophones, and homographs. I couldn't stop imagining what awful thing had happened to Owen. Finally, it was recess. We spilled out into the hall and were swept out to the playground with all the other kids.

Maya flashed her hockey cards. "Here, I'll show you my best ones."

I looked down at her collection — mostly Canucks players.

"We could make some trades if you want to," she said.

"Maybe. But I'm not much of a Canucks fan."

"Not yet." She smiled.

Trying not to sound too eager, I finally asked, "So, what were you going to tell me about Owen?"

Maya's face turned serious. "Oh, poor Owen." She shuffled her cards. "Ever notice how parents are always saying stuff like 'Don't play with matches' or 'Never talk to strangers' or 'Look both ways when you cross the street'?"

"Yeah. So did he get burned? Kidnapped? Hit by a car?"

"No, nothing like that. I was just thinking about how parents always warn you about stuff that could happen if you're not careful, but you never listen 'cause you think they're just trying to scare you."

I tried to appear patient, but inside I was wondering if she was ever going to get to the point.

"You don't know this about him, but Owen is a science geek, like his dad. They like to make things together: robots, rockets, fireworks. At the start of summer holidays, he and a few friends went down to the train tracks."

"Parents always say, 'Never play on the train tracks,'" I blurted. "That's it, isn't it? Owen got hurt playing on the tracks."

"Not exactly."

"Okay, then," I said, "how'd he get hurt?"

"Well, if you'd let me talk without interrupting …" Then she paused like she wanted to be dramatic and all.

I tapped my foot impatiently.

"So, like I was saying, Owen and his dad like to make things, like fireworks. Hmm, I just thought of another thing parents say: 'Never set off fireworks without an adult present.'"

I gasped. "He let off fireworks without his dad?" That was dangerous! Cool, but definitely dangerous.

"Yeah, he and some boys went down to the tracks to set off some of Owen's homemade Roman candles — ones he and his dad made, leftover from last Halloween. Someone got the idea to tie them to the tracks and then wait for the train to run over them, to see if the heat and friction would ignite them. It was a bad idea, but, I admit, it would have been spectacular — if it had worked the way they thought it was going to." She stopped and shuffled her card collection.

I gritted my teeth and squirmed. I had to pee bad but I wanted to hear the end of the story.

"Well, they waited and waited and finally the passenger train to Seattle went by. But nothing happened."

I groaned. "Nothing happened? Okay, this is starting to sound like you're just pulling my leg."

"Not at all. When the Roman candles didn't go off, Owen went over to see why. I guess there was a delayed reaction or something 'cause suddenly those fireworks lit up. They burned Owen's hands and face real bad. But worse, one of the Roman candles ripped into his foot." She paused while that sank in and then added, "The doctors had to amputate it."

My breath escaped through my lips in a loud whoosh. "His foot?"

Maya nodded sadly.

"That's awful," I whispered, almost wishing she hadn't told me. "Is he going to be okay?"

28

Maya looked gloomy. "Mrs. Bradshaw told my dad that Owen is doing better and the burns are healing, but he has a lot of bad dreams about the accident. He doesn't want to come to school yet." She picked up a shiny pebble from the ground and rolled it around in her hand. Then she sighed. "Guess there won't be a neighbourhood fireworks show this year."

"Fireworks show?" I asked.

"Yeah, it's been a tradition around here for as long as I can remember. The Bradshaw family lights off all their fireworks — mostly ones Owen's dad makes — on Halloween night. Everyone brings lawn chairs and blankets and parks on their front lawn to watch. But after what happened to Owen, I'm pretty sure that's over."

"That's too bad," I said. Poor Owen. I thought about him swimming in his pool the other day. It had sounded like he was really struggling. Guess so, with only one foot. It was weird — I kind of missed him, even though we'd never even met. If I'd been more like Bennie, I would have gone over to his house by now to introduce myself. I had more questions to ask Maya, but it was time to go back to class.

★　✱　★

At lunch I wandered over to watch some guys play ball hockey. It used to be my favourite game at my old school. Danny was there. It was annoying to admit, but he was really good. He deked like a pro, and popped the ball in the net easy as a hot knife slices butter.

"Good thing you're not wearing that lousy Leafs jersey," Danny said when he saw me watching. "You play?"

"Me?" My heart skipped a beat. "Yeah, a little. Goalie mostly."

"Hey, Andy, this kid here wants your job!" said Danny to the boy in goal.

"Never said that," I quickly replied. My cheeks got hot, and my muscles tensed.

"Yeah, right. Like to see him try," said Andy, shaking his stick.

"Okay, that's it. Everyone, line up," shouted Danny. "We're taking shots on goal to see what the new guy's got." He grabbed the goalie stick from Andy and tossed it to me.

"Suit up, kid."

I thought about protesting, but it was clear Danny was the kind of guy who always got what he wanted. "Sure, since you insist," I said. He shot me a glare that looked like a warning.

As I pulled on the goalie pads and mask, I noticed a lot of kids had stopped their own games and joined the crowd. Probably hoping to see Danny and his pals stomp all over me. I walked slowly to the net, trying to get a feel for the stick. It had been a while since I'd played. I was doing a few lunges to stretch out my legs when I heard a familiar voice call out. I cringed.

"C'mon, Wart. You can do it," shouted Bennie from the sidelines. Maya stood beside him. "You're the best goalie in the world," he said.

I watched kids look from me to Bennie and then back to me. Then came an explosion of laughter and chanting. "Wart! Wart! Wart!" Of course, Bennie thought it was great and joined them. I tried getting his attention to make him stop, but the other kids were too into it now.

"Hey, you want me to shut the little goofball up?" said Danny, looking down on Bennie.

"You shut up, Danny. That's his brother!" Maya spouted. "Wart's his nickname."

"Yeah, they're twins," said Maya's brother, Taylor. What was most annoying was how he smirked from ear to ear.

Danny stepped back and pretended to study Bennie, then me. "Oh, right. Now I see it. Identical twins? Right? Ha!"

And just like that, I went from being Warren, potentially cool new kid at the school, to Bennie's brother, Wart. And like so often lately, I lost it. "Hey, jerk, we've all got things to do. Are you going to just stand there, or you going to shoot?" I barked.

Danny looked surprised, then grinned. "You got it, Wart!"

By the time the bell rang ten minutes later, I'd stopped nineteen out of twenty-one shots on goal. I had to admit the adrenalin mixed with anger probably had something to do with it. All the kids watching started back to class. A bunch said stuff to me like "Way to go," "Nice job," and "You were rocking."

Danny walked up to me. "Not bad … Wart!" he teased. "You should come out to play with us on Saturday."

I threw off the gear and started to head back to class. "Probably not." I would have liked to see the look on his face, but didn't dare look back.

"Good job, Wart. Knew you could do it," called Bennie. The problem was he kept chanting "Wart, Wart, Wart!" as Maya walked him back to class.

I couldn't stand it. I ran over and grabbed him by the shirt. Through gritted teeth I said to Maya, "Next time you want to play with Bennie, don't bring him over here." Then I looked at Bennie, whose eyes had grown to the size of toonies. "And you're not supposed to call me Wart in public. How many times do you need to be told?"

I didn't wait for either of them to reply. I just turned and went back to class.

All afternoon I could feel Maya's angry eyes on me. I bet if she were a dragon she'd have been breathing fire. I didn't care. Because if I'd been a dragon, she'd have been deep-fried!

* * *

That night after supper, Dad banged on the table. "Okay, gang. It's Friday night. What do you say we all go to the pool for family swim?"

Bennie sprang from his chair and ran around the kitchen yahooing. Then he took off to his bedroom. "C'mon, Wart, help me find my swimsuit!"

Mom gave me a funny look. "I'll help you, dear. We can't always be asking Warren for help — apparently."

"Warren, everything okay? You don't seem too enthusiastic," said Dad.

I sighed. "Just missing our old place, I guess. I wish Michael was here and could come with us to the pool."

"Is that what's been on your mind all through supper? I could see something was bothering you."

I didn't feel like talking about what had happened at school, so I let him think my bad mood was all about missing Michael.

Dad pulled my chair closer to him and put his arm around my shoulders. "Having a brother with special needs can be demanding, Warren. So much of our time has been focused on Bennie, taking him to specialists, figuring out our next step to make life better for him. Even our move out here was so we could improve his quality of life."

"I know, Dad. And I want things to be good for him."

"Of course you do, Warren. You're a good brother. But it must have been hard for you when we hauled you across the country, making you leave your old school and friends behind. But I promise things are going to get better soon. And this is going to be your year, pal. Hey, maybe we can finally get you on to a soccer or hockey team. How about that?"

I shrugged. "Yeah, that would be cool."

"In the meantime, what do you say? Come swimming?" He grabbed me at the waist and started tickling and wrestling with me. "Say you'll come to the pool and have fun with us. Come on, say it!"

What could I do? I either had to give in or die laughing. Besides, I was starting to feel better and knew swimming would be fun.

"Okay, okay. I give. I'll go." Dad let me go after messing my hair, and I ran off to get ready.

* * *

"Wart, we're down here. We're watchin'," Bennie called, as I stood at the end of the high diving board. I was glad to see Dad correcting him. I was still kind of mad at him for today, but could tell he'd forgotten all about how I yelled at him. He was like that. He didn't hang on to stuff, never held a grudge, and he hardly ever got mad at people.

I edged to the tip of the board, bent my legs, and sprang hard and high. When my head popped back out of the water, my family was cheering like I was an Olympic athlete or something. As I swam toward them, Bennie doggy-paddled over to meet me. When he started guzzling half the pool and began to sink, I grabbed him by the arm and swung him onto my back, then swam back to Mom and Dad.

"You were great. You should be a professional diver — after you become a professional hockey player, and soccer player, too. I hope I can be like you one day," Bennie said, squeezing me tight.

I guess you could say we were having one of those twin moments, because my heart was suddenly too big for my chest and I squeezed him back.

After that we played and had a couple races, and Bennie and I crawled onto Dad so he could throw us off into the water. Then we had an underwater breath-holding contest, and I beat everyone. We were having a good time and I'd finally forgotten about what had happened at school earlier. When it was time to go, neither Bennie nor I wanted to leave.

"Come on, out of the pool, guys," Dad said. I reluctantly climbed out along with my parents. But Bennie wouldn't budge.

"Come on, Bennie," said Mom. "It's time to go." Bennie sheepishly shook his head and refused to get out of the pool.

"That's enough, sport. Get out of the pool *now*," ordered Dad. Bennie slowly climbed the ladder. As he did, I noticed some kids staring at him and snickering. I was getting madder by the second — until I saw what they were laughing about.

"Bennie, where's your bathing suit?" Mom asked, quickly guiding my bare-bummed brother toward the family changing room.

"I don't know, Mom. It fell off," he said, his cheeks pink. "I was just havin' so much fun, I didn't notice. Please don't be mad, Mom."

Mom laughed. "Oh, honey, never mind. We'll get Warren to find it." She turned to me. "Would you please try to find his bathing suit?"

I looked back at the sea of smirking faces staring at us. Some kid in the bleachers aimed a cellphone at my brother.

"Forget it, I'm not doing it. Dad can." I bolted off to the change room.

Like always, the fiasco was laughed off. Everyone chattered in the car all the way home — everyone except me. I shrank down in my seat.

"I'm tired. Going to bed," I announced when we got in the house.

"What about ice cream, Wart? We always have ice cream on Friday nights," said Bennie, running for the kitchen.

"Don't want any."

In bed, I replayed in my mind the scene of my brother streaking bare-bummed into the change room, and I saw again all those grinning faces. I remembered the guy taking pictures and knew there was a good chance they were already posted on social media. *Wouldn't be surprised if some kids from school have already seen them*, I thought. I rolled over and buried my head under the pillow.

The thing was, even if Bennie hadn't done something spectacularly embarrassing, like losing his swimsuit, there would have been someone gawking — someone curious about him or feeling sorry. Like the night we went for pizza, some old people stared while the waitress led us to our booth. I heard the lady say, "Aw, look at the poor little fellow. So sad to see children like that." I wanted to knock her drink onto her lap. But all I could do was stare back until she got uncomfortable and stopped looking at us. Why did she think he was a poor little fellow? He was the happiest person I knew, and unlike me, he didn't give a squat what other people thought about him.

"Warren, are you still awake?" Mom stood in the doorway with the light from the hall casting her shadow over the floor.

I didn't want to talk so I didn't answer.

"I know you're upset about what happened at the pool. But honey, one day you'll look back and laugh over it."

I still didn't say anything.

"Okay, let's talk about this in the morning. Just remember one thing for me: It's hard for people to laugh at you when you're laughing with them."

Sure, easy for her to say. She and Dad never seemed to notice or even care about those people who were laughing. No, that was my problem. My whole life, I was either trying to protect my brother or feeling embarrassed by the things he said or did. Whichever it was, no one else in my family noticed or even cared.

CHAPTER 4

When I woke on Saturday morning, the house was filled with a delicious smell. Normally, Bennie would have been jumping all over me by now, begging me to come and watch cartoons. Instead, I got to sleep in.

I walked into the living room. Bennie was sitting quietly on the floor, with three of his jigsaw puzzles spread out over the carpet, each one half-done. Here was a kid who couldn't read or tie his shoelaces, but for some reason could see almost instantly how a bunch of tiny puzzle pieces fit together. Lots of times I'd seen him put a 250-piece jigsaw puzzle together in under twenty minutes. That was why he always did two or three at the same time. One was too easy.

"Hi, Wart," Bennie said, jumping up from the floor to give me a hug.

"Hi," I answered and squeezed him back.

"Mom, Wart's awake. Can we eat breakfast now? Mom made you a surprise. Come and see," Bennie urged.

In the kitchen I saw a big plate of pancakes at my spot. Each had blueberry eyes, a strawberry nose, and slices of banana in the shape of a big smile.

"Mom says they're not pancakes — they're man-cakes! Ha! Get it?" said Bennie.

I grinned and nodded.

"C'mon, Wart, eat. Want some syrup on them? Or peanut butter?" He always looked hopeful, like one day I'd actually go for it.

I looked at my mom, who was smiling. "Thanks," I said. "This looks great. Think I'll pass on the pea-nut butter and just have syrup."

"I hope you're feeling better," Mom said. I had been, until her question reminded me about every-thing that had happened the day before.

"I'm fine," I said.

"Good. Dig in while the pancakes are hot." Just as I took my first bite, the doorbell rang. "You go ahead. I'll see who it is," said Mom.

A minute later Mom walked back into the kitchen, followed by Maya. "Look who's here, boys," Mom said.

I nearly dropped my fork. Worse, I realized I was still in my pyjamas — the old Spider-Man ones with holes in the knees. As my cheeks burned

I wondered, *Does she even know how lousy her timing is?*

My brother ran over and hugged her.

"Thanks, Bennie. Hi, Warren." Maya waved. "Hey, I can come back later when you're finished breakfast."

"That's okay. We don't mind, do we, boys? Would you like some pancakes, Maya?" Mom didn't wait for an answer. She just started piling some on a plate and set them on the table.

Maya dug right in, as though dropping in on my family on a Saturday morning was completely normal and I hadn't yelled at her the day before. I wondered what she thought as she looked at us all. Mom's hair looked like she'd just had shock treatment, Bennie was nearly covered from head to toe in syrup and peanut butter, and I was wearing my ratty, too-small Spider-Man PJs. Funny how one minute we were just being our normal Saturday-morning selves and the next we were a family of dorks.

"These are the best pancakes," Maya said, her cheeks bulging.

"Really? Well, thank you, Maya. But I'm sure they're just as good as your mother's," Mom said.

"Maybe, but I don't remember. She died when I was five." There was an awkward silence for a couple of seconds. I tried to think of something nice to say.

"Bet her pancakes were super-duper delicious, Maya. Just as good as my mom's," said Bennie. "Do you got a dad who can make pancakes?" And just like that the awkward moment passed.

"My dad's good at lots of things, but not at cooking. His one specialty is spaghetti and meatballs."

"Shluppp! I love spaghetti and meatballs. Don't I, Mom?" Bennie licked his lips.

Mom smiled. "You certainly do. Not as much as peanut butter and pickle sandwiches. But it's right up there with your favourites." She turned to Maya. "Do you have siblings, Maya?"

"Yes, I have a younger brother, Taylor." She looked at me for a second and then down at her plate. She ran her finger over the last of the syrup and then licked it off.

"Here, have a couple more pancakes," said Mom. Again she piled them onto Maya's plate without waiting for a response. "Since they're so good."

"Thanks, Mrs. Osborne!" Maya really did seem to be enjoying them.

"When you're finished, you wanna help me with my puzzles?" asked Bennie.

Between mouthfuls Maya mumbled, "Sure, Bennie, I'll help you."

I was glad now that Maya had come over and that she got to have pancakes with us. Having no mom would be hard. When she followed Bennie into the living room a few minutes later, I tore off for my bedroom and threw on my shirt and jeans.

"Is Warren doing one of these puzzles, too?" I heard her ask my brother.

"Nope. He doesn't do puzzles. He likes hockey and soccer," said Bennie.

"So why are there so many on the floor? Who's doing the other ones?"

"I am," said Bennie.

"All three? At the same time?" She looked at me as I walked into the room. "Bennie says he's doing all three puzzles."

I grinned. "Yeah, that's right. It's what he does. He's a jigsaw puzzle junkie. He can do puzzles like these really easily, so he does three at a time to make it more challenging." I walked over to the hall closet and opened it to show another forty or so puzzle boxes. Most of them were 250 pieces. "My parents are always going to garage sales to get him new ones."

"Wow! That's cool, Bennie. You're talented."

Bennie didn't hear her because he was already sitting on the floor with his nose in a pile of puzzle pieces. His hands were flying around at warp speed, sticking tiny cardboard bits into place.

Maya looked at me. "That's pretty amazing. He should be on TV or something."

TV? Ha! Nobody would want to watch some kid doing puzzles on TV. That would be as bad as watching *Antiques Roadshow* or golf.

"Here, Maya, you do that one." Bennie pointed to a puzzle of outer space. "That's my favourite." It was almost entirely black except for a few specks of white that were supposed to be stars. I wanted to laugh out loud. I'd tried doing that one with him once. It was hopeless. I doubted she'd be able to fit a single piece in place before he finished the other two — and sure enough, I was right.

"Do you want to do something after this?" Maya asked, giving up on the puzzle.

"I heard some of the guys are going to the park to play ball hockey," I said. "Think I'll go."

"Oh. I guess we could go and watch. Is that okay with you, Bennie?"

He didn't answer because he was fitting in the last few pieces of the outer space puzzle. "Done!" he said.

Maya looked surprised and then laughed. "That's amazing. Good thing I was here to help you, right?"

"Yup. Good thing." Five seconds after finishing, Bennie was pulling the puzzles apart and throwing the pieces back into the boxes.

"Wait! What are you doing?" Maya looked alarmed. "You just finished those. Don't you want to look at them for a while, or show your parents?"

"Nope. Mom said I got to clean up after I'm done. Besides, I'm gonna make 'em again later. Let's go," Bennie said.

"Go where?" said Maya.

"To watch Wart play hockey."

"You heard that? I didn't think you were listening," said Maya, smiling.

No way are they coming, I thought. I didn't want a repeat of the day before. "It's a free world, but I think Bennie would rather play *The Walking Dead*. Right, Bennie?"

"Yeah!" Bennie jumped up and down. "That would be more fun. Let's do it, guys. Let's play *The Walking Dead*."

"Okay," Maya said. "Let's see who else we can find to play. And this time I'll be the zombie."

"Okay." Bennie ran to the closet and threw on his jacket. "C'mon, Wart. Let's go."

"Nah, not me. I'm going to play ball hockey," I said.

Maya frowned. I could see she wanted to say something, but Mom walked into the room.

"Hang on there, mister. You can't go out looking like that," Mom said. "You go and get dressed first."

Bennie looked down at his Mickey Mouse pyjamas and laughed. "Ha. I forgot. Thanks, Mom." Then he padded off to get changed.

I put on my socks and grabbed my jacket. I wanted to get out of there as fast as I could — and alone.

"You know, Danny is probably going to be there," Maya said.

"Yeah, probably. So what?"

"Oh, nothing really. I just didn't think he was the kind of kid you'd want to hang out with. Especially after he made fun of Bennie and you."

"Look, I just like to play ball hockey. Sounds like you're the one who has a problem with him."

Maya's cheeks turned pink. "Not a problem for me. Play with whoever you want." Then a moment later her face turned soft. "Actually, Danny needs a good friend like you. Things are hard for him at home. It's probably what made him …" She paused, looking for the right word.

"Made him what?" I asked.

"An insensitive, selfish jerk. I don't want to hang out with him, but he's lucky that you don't mind."

I shrugged. "Whatever. Like I said, it's just ball hockey. I'm not going to make him my best friend."

She was studying the picture on one of the puzzle boxes. "Well, don't be surprised if that's how it looks to everyone else."

Now she was just being annoying. "I'm going now, Maya. You have fun playing *The Walking Dead* and maybe I'll see you later."

★　★　★

"I wonder when old one-foot Owen is coming back to school. He must feel like such a freak," Danny said. He took a slapshot on the net. I stopped him short and passed the ball to Jesse to send down to the other end of the court.

"Nice one, Wart," said Danny. I hated it when he called me that, but there was no way I was going to let him know it.

"Do you think he'll be able to play hockey again? He was so good," said Jesse.

Danny came up behind and checked him hard and snagged the ball. Jesse fell onto the pavement, scraping his hand. He winced and clutched it to his chest. "Why did you check me so hard?"

"Oh no, poor Jesse has a boo-boo." Danny laughed. "Gotta be tough to play this game." He whipped over to the side to get some water, leaving the ball just sitting there.

Helping Jesse up, I whispered, "Quick, grab it and send it down the sideline while he's not looking." Jesse nodded. In a flash he took off with the ball, and slapped it past Andy for a goal before Danny even knew what was happening.

Of course, Danny whined about it for the rest of the game, saying it wasn't fair to shoot the ball while he was taking a water break. He said the goal didn't count, but we knew it did.

"Too bad Owen wasn't here," Jesse said after we lost the game five to three. We were sitting together on the grass. The others had gone home. "He's the only one that could beat Danny. He was the best player in the school."

A guy who was a great hockey player, could make things blow up, and had a swimming pool — that was the kind of guy I really wanted to know. "I sure hope he'll still be able to play," I said.

"I hope so, too. But it will probably be pretty hard with his fake foot and all," Jesse said. As he sat bending his plastic hockey blade, I could tell there was something more he wanted to say. "It's going to be weird seeing him when he finally comes back to school."

"Why?"

"Because it'll be the first time we've seen him since it happened," he said, real quiet.

"Since the accident? Were you there?" I asked. Dread trickled down my spine.

"Yeah. We all were." Jesse's voice was shaky.

"Really? When the rocket went off? That must have been awful." I cringed just thinking about it.

"Yeah, it was. At first everyone was screaming and crying. No one knew what to do. But then I managed to remember things I learned from the babysitter's first-aid class I had to take, like applying pressure and telling Andy and David to go for help."

"What did Danny do?" I asked.

"Danny? He didn't do anything. He was like a frozen statue. Wet his pants, that's how scared he was. Now he jokes about it like it was no big deal. But we saw him."

*   *   *

I rode slowly back home, thinking about the things Jesse told me. I wondered what made guys like Owen brave and guys like Danny mean. Maya said things weren't good at Danny's house. I'd heard that kids who are bullied at home sometimes become bullies, too. Was that what made him such a schmuck?

"Where's Bennie?" I asked Mom as I walked into the kitchen. "Maya go home?"

"No. They're both just over there." It looked like she was pointing to the backyard.

I looked out the kitchen window. "I don't see them."

"Not our backyard," she said. "There, over the fence, at the neighbours' house."

"Wha—" My voice cracked. "Well, when?"

"Oh, I don't know, not long after you left. They couldn't get anyone to play their game." Mom looked up from her laptop.

"So, what, they just went there without being invited? You know that kid had a bad accident. Maybe his mom —"

"Hold the phone, kiddo. Maya called first. And I even spoke to the boy's mom. So it's fine, Warren." She poured herself some coffee.

"Ah, well, shouldn't you call Bennie home for lunch?"

Mom looked at me like I was cracked. "He's fine, Warren. And you know him — if he gets hungry he'll come home. Besides, I'm sure Maya will bring him back when they've worn out their welcome." She took a sip of her coffee. "But if you're concerned about it, I'm sure it would be fine if you went over there to check on him." She headed for her office.

I sat at the kitchen table, staring out the window at the Bradshaws' house. I could only see the second floor over the hedge, but there was no mistaking the voices and sounds of people splashing in the pool. It reminded me how hot it was, especially for a mid-September Saturday, and how nice a swim would be.

I really wanted to go over to Owen's house, and I was trying to think of what cool thing I could say when I showed up at his door. *Hi, I'm Bennie's brother. Can I come and play, too?* No way — that sounded juvenile. If only Maya had told me she was going to Owen's place, I might have stayed home from hockey.

Just then I heard the front door open. "Mom, I need a towel," Bennie yelled. "I'm soakin' wet."

"Warren, get your brother a towel, please. I'm busy," called Mom.

"Here," I said, throwing a towel down the stairs at him. "Where you been?"

"I been at my new friend's house. His name's Owen and he lives behind us, on the other side of the fence."

"Huh," I said, trying not to sound too interested. "You going back there? I could go with you."

"Nope. His mom said he needs to rest now. Know why I'm all wet?"

"You peed yourself?"

"No!" Bennie giggled. "It's 'cause I been in Owen's pool."

"Oh yeah?" I tried not to care, but I did.

"It's a real nice pool, Wart. You'd like it. And 'nother thing, Owen has puzzles. Lots of 'em. And he said I could put 'em together."

My ears were hot and I could feel the trickle of sweat down my back. "Sounds boring. You've got lots of your own puzzles."

"Not boring at all. He's got puzzles I never seen before. Like ones that make shapes. Those are my favourite."

"Shapes? You mean like 3-D puzzles?"

"I dunno, what's that?" Bennie asked.

"Never mind. Either way it's just another puzzle," I said. I turned on the TV to find something to watch.

"'Nother thing, Owen's mom made chocolate-chip cookies and let me put peanut butter on 'em, too. Everyone thought it made 'em more delicious. So did I."

"Better than Mom's cookies? Doubt it." I flicked through the channels faster and faster, annoyed there was nothing good on.

"I like Mom's cookies. I like 'em a lot. And I like Owen's mom's cookies. Both are good." Bennie pulled off his wet bathing suit and flung it down the hall toward his room.

"Whoa! Cover up, dude," I told him. He wrapped the towel around himself but it was too late. I'd seen it. Gross. "Maya and Owen did puzzles, too? 'Cause if they did, that would have been boring. Glad I wasn't there."

"Nope." He leaned in like he had a secret. "Maya isn't too good at puzzles. Don't tell her I said that. I don't wanna hurt her feelings."

"So you did puzzles — something you do at home. You ate cookies — something you can have at home. And you went swimming. Did your bathing suit fall off in the pool again?"

Bennie's cheeks turned pink and his chin fell. "Nope. Didn't lose it. Not at all, Wart. I promise."

It felt like I'd just stabbed myself in the heart. "Well, glad you had a nice time," I said, trying to sound nicer than I felt.

"Oh, I forgot. One more thing, Owen has a robot," Bennie said.

"Like a toy robot? Big deal. I had one of those once."

"Nope, not a toy. It's big, bigger than me. They call it Reggie — yup, Reggie the Robot. It lives in the garage. That's where Owen and his dad like to make things. It rolls around and talks. I don't like that. It scares me, Wart. More than zombies. Oh, I nearly forgot somethin.'" He handed me a damp hockey card. "Owen said to give you this." I gulped. It was a replica of Warren Godfrey, one of the best former defenceman for the Detroit Red Wings. "His name is Warren, just like you. Good, eh?"

My eyes lit up. This was the chance I'd been looking for. "Cool. I better go over and thank him right away," I said, heading for the door.

"Nope. Better not," Bennie said. "His mom said Owen's had enough for today."

Disappointment washed over me and I sat on the sofa picking at a few loose threads on my pants. Soon I'd made a hole big enough to fit two fingers.

★　★　★

On Monday I got to school early. I wanted to be sitting in my desk when Owen arrived. Soon the room filled with kids, but still he didn't come. As Mrs. Chapman closed the door, I leaned across the aisle and whispered to Maya. "Where's Owen? I figured he'd be here today."

"No. He's still not ready to come to school," she said.

"Really? If the guy can play with you and Bennie most of Saturday, he's got to be ready to go to school. Wish I could skip out whenever I felt like it."

"It's not like that, Warren," said Maya. She looked annoyed.

"Isn't it? He's not worried about getting too far behind?" I said.

"Mrs. Chapman sends him stuff. Besides, he's pretty smart."

"Smart enough to miss school, that's for sure." I didn't know why I was feeling bothered. I just was.

"Of all people, I thought you'd be more sensitive." Maya's top lip curled up when she looked at me.

"Why?" I stared back hard. "Because of Bennie? That's ridiculous, Maya. I thought *you'd* be more sensitive."

"I'm not talking about that! Think about how you'd feel if all of a sudden you couldn't play ball hockey anymore, or soccer, or run, or even walk without a limp, or without it hurting? And that's not all. He still gets nervous at loud noises and his face has scars."

"Oh," I said quietly. My cheeks burned. I turned and faced the front of the room and vowed to keep my mouth shut about Owen Bradshaw.

CHAPTER 5

September turned into October, and Owen's desk was still empty. I didn't hear him in his backyard, either. It was too cold outside to swim. Lots of times I thought about going over to say hi and thank him for the hockey card, but I always lost my nerve. I was never any good at being the first to talk to new people — I wasn't like Bennie. Besides, after what Maya said, I didn't want to bother him. If it had been me, I wouldn't want some kid I didn't know knocking on my door to say hello.

Just before the start of the Thanksgiving long weekend, Mrs. Chapman posted two notices on our class bulletin board. "I want you all to take a look at this volunteer list. As you know, the grade sixes and sevens are expected to do service work for the school." A few kids groaned. "Now, that's enough of that. Everyone needs to sign up for at least one activity. Miss Jones needs a minimum of five helpers to assist with the children in her class." She looked right at me. "Perhaps this would be something you'd be interested in."

And why would you think that? I thought.

"I'll do it," Maya piped up. "We could volunteer together, Warren."

"Maybe," I mumbled.

"The other thing I want to announce," continued Mrs. Chapman, "is that our annual Halloween costume parade and talent show will be at the end of the month."

Some kids started squealing like piglets, and others were jumping up and down in their seats.

"Okay, okay. Settle down," said Mrs. Chapman. She had to raise her voice above the ruckus. "That's not too far away, so start giving some thought to what you're going to wear for the parade and what you want to do for the talent show."

Mrs. Chapman tried her best to settle the class down, but in the end she dismissed us early to go home for the long weekend.

"I'm going to dress up as a magician," said Maya as we rode home on our bikes. "I've got some great magic tricks I've been practising. What about you, Warren?"

"Me? I'm really good at playing 'Jingle Bells' on my armpit," I said. "Think that counts as a talent?"

Maya howled and bounced up and down on her bike seat. "That will be totally funny."

I laughed at her foolishness. "I'm not serious, though. I'd never do it."

She looked at me like I'd lost my mind. "Why not? Everyone will laugh."

"But what if they don't? What if they think it's boring and throw rotten tomatoes? No. Not doing it," I told her.

"You know, Warren, you take yourself too seriously," Maya said. I didn't like being judged and looked away at the houses we were passing. "You should learn to relax, like Bennie. Speaking of which, he should totally sign up for the talent show, too."

I shot her a quick look to see if she was joking, but from what I could tell she was serious. "And do what? Puzzles?" Now that would be seriously boring.

"Yeah, of course. The way he does jigsaw puzzles is an amazing talent," she said.

I almost wanted to scream at her. Maya had no idea what she was talking about or what something like that could do to Bennie — or to me. "No, it's not. It's puzzles. It'll be lame, and kids will make fun of him."

"There you go again, worrying about what other people will think or do. Well, I'm going to ask him if he wants to sign up," Maya said defiantly.

Not if I have anything to do with it, I thought.

★　★　★

The next morning when I walked into the kitchen, Bennie was eating, as usual. "Mornin', Wart," he mumbled. "Want some?" He offered me a piece of his toast slathered in peanut butter and topped with sliced pickles.

"Bennie, you know I don't eat peanut butter and pickles. So why do you keep asking me?"

He smiled up at me. "Just thinkin' you might change your mind someday." Then he stuffed the rest of his toast into his mouth.

Dad wandered into the kitchen. "Good morning, boys." He stretched and let out a huge yawn. "Nice to have a sleep-in, eh?"

"What are we gonna do today?" asked Bennie, wiping his mouth on his pyjamas.

"Oh, I don't know. How about we just laze around, watch some TV? Maybe have a nap." Dad slumped down into a chair and propped his chin on his hand.

"Aw, Dad. That doesn't sound good at all," Bennie whined. "Did you know Teacher says we gotta get a costume for the Halloween parade at school? Do I have a costume, Dad? 'Cause Teacher says I gotta."

Dad looked at me. "What's he talking about?"

I rolled my eyes. "Yeah, my teacher said the same thing. The school always has a Halloween parade.

And —" I sighed "— a talent show. But there's no way I'm going to do that. And just in case Maya mentions it, don't let her sign Bennie up, either."

"Sign him up to do what?" asked Dad. The doorbell rang. "Hold that thought while I answer the door."

"Let me, let me," sang Bennie. "I'll answer the door. And I know, don't let any strangers in."

When Bennie had left the kitchen, Dad said, "So what's this about a talent show?"

"Maya's got it in her head that Bennie could do a puzzle for the talent show. I told her it was a bad idea. But she won't listen to me, so you should tell her to back off."

He ran his fingers through his hair. "Well, I don't know, maybe she's on to something. It is kind of superhuman the way he does puzzles. I don't know anyone who's as good as your brother. Do you?" said Dad.

"No, but that's because nobody does jigsaw puzzles anymore. And besides, don't you think he gets stared at enough as it is? If he gets up in front of the whole school to do a puzzle, he'll look like a clown. Dad, do you really want him to be a target for kids who'll make fun of him?" I didn't bother to mention how bad it would make me look.

Dad leaned in and patted my arm. "I know there have been times in the past, but don't you think by now —"

"No, Dad. I know what I'm talking about." I could feel my cheeks burn when my dad frowned.

But I didn't care. He wasn't the one who had to go to school every day and face all those judging eyes.

The conversation stopped when Bennie ran back into the kitchen. "Hey, everybody, look who's here."

Maya walked through the door, carrying a tablet under her arm. I was in my pyjamas again! Only this time I was wearing my Superman PJs with the torn pocket. I should have known she'd show up un-announced. It was becoming her habit.

"Hi, Mr. Osborne," Maya said. "Is this a good time?"

"Sure it is, Maya. That is, if you don't mind how we're dressed," said Dad.

Maya bent over to look at my PJs from bottom to top. "Nice, Warren. Superman, eh? I think I like the Spider-Man ones better." She laughed.

"Ah, they're old," I mumbled. "Gotta get some new ones." *She's so annoying*, I thought.

"Mom," Bennie called. "Maya's here. Can you make pancakes for her?"

"Shh, Bennie. Don't say that." She looked at me for help. "Really, that's not why I came over."

Her face looked funny when it was all red. "Ha. Payback!" She looked at me, confused. "Never mind," I said, crossing my arms over my chest to hide my ripped pocket.

"Hello, Maya. Did I hear someone was request-ing pancakes?" said Mom, strolling into the kitchen.

She stretched her arms up to the ceiling and gave a Saturday-morning yawn even louder than Dad's, and then shook it out like a hairy dog that's just come out of the lake. "Sorry about that."

"Yup," said Bennie. "I think Maya needs some more pancakes. You know how her dad's not good at cookin', so you should make her some. Pleeease." Bennie begged like a puppy. Mom snickered.

"Bennie, no." Maya looked like she wanted to melt into the floor. "Sorry, Mrs. Osborne. I didn't come here to have pancakes."

"Oh well, that's too bad," said Dad, "because I haven't had pancakes in a long time and would enjoy some." He grabbed my mom around the waist and hugged her.

"I'll make you a deal," said Mom. "I'll do the pancakes and you do the dishes."

"Done," said Dad. "Boys, you heard your mother. After pancakes you do the dishes."

"Very funny, mister. I was talking to you." Mom bopped him on the head lightly with the frying pan. "Sorry, Maya. Looks like you're having pancakes again." Maya smiled shyly and Bennie danced around the kitchen.

Maya set her tablet on the table. "Warren, I want to show you something." She opened up the webpage for the *Guinness World Records*. "Read it."

I leaned over to have a look.

"What is it?" Bennie asked her.

"It's talking about a fifteen-year-old girl in Connecticut who is the fastest puzzler in the world. She did a two-hundred-fifty-piece jigsaw puzzle in just over thirteen minutes," Maya told him.

"Really! There's actually a category for puzzle making? Let me have a look at that," said Dad, taking the tablet from me. He scrolled down the page. "Huh. Says here she can assemble nineteen pieces a minute. Amazing."

"Is that fast, Dad?" Bennie asked.

"You bet. It's Superman fast, or Road Runner fast," Dad said.

"Oh boy, that's fast," Bennie echoed. I liked how Dad always put things in a way that helped my brother to understand.

Maya beamed. "Bet you're just as fast, Bennie."

What a sneak! "Aw, Bennie doesn't care about stuff like that. So what if that kid is fast, right, Bennie?"

"Is that what I am, Dad, a puzzler?" my brother asked, totally ignoring me.

"I guess so. I've never heard it put like that before," Dad said, passing the tablet back to me.

Bennie's chest puffed up. "Hey, Wart, I'm a puzzler. How do you like them apples?" My parents laughed as he strutted around the kitchen like a flat-footed peacock. Then he climbed onto Dad's lap.

Maya looked at me, and I gave her the stink eye. "Nice try. Now back off," I mouthed so only she could see.

She ignored me and said, "When did you first start doing puzzles, Bennie?"

Bennie looked at Dad and shrugged. "I don't know. Dad, do you know?"

"I think you were … what, six? It was actually Warren's puzzle, but he didn't want it. So one day we came into your bedroom and there you were, sitting on the floor, and the puzzle was all done. At first I thought maybe Warren had put it together. But no, it was you."

"So you could say it was Warren's fault for getting Bennie hooked on puzzles," said Maya. My parents laughed and Bennie clapped his hands.

"Yup, all your fault, Wart." Bennie giggled. "All 'cause you didn't like the *101 Dalmatians*!"

"That was your first puzzle? That's crazy. I've got goosebumps," Maya said, her eyes as big as golf balls.

I started setting out plates and condiments. "You're weird, Maya. It was only a little kids' puzzle. Had only fifty pieces," I said.

"Yeah, but it just so happens that was the first puzzle Deepika did when she was little," said Maya. "Don't you find that odd?"

"And who's Deepika?" I sighed. I was getting tired of this conversation fast.

"Her, the girl in the *Guinness World Records*." Maya lowered her voice. "It's like an omen or something. Bennie, I think you could beat her record one day."

I couldn't believe it. My parents were doing nothing, saying nothing. What was wrong with them? "Don't be filling his head with stuff like that," I said.

Mom threw the soggy dishcloth at me and stared hard. That hurt in more ways than one.

"What? I'm just saying Bennie's not like Deepika."

"You just wait and see, Warren. I think he's going to be the next jigsaw puzzle king! You said it yourself: he's a jigsaw junkie." Maya looked very pleased with herself. Man, she was more annoying than a room full of blackflies.

"You never know," Dad said, smiling at Bennie. "You just never know."

Was I the only sane person in the room? The only one who could see the problem in all this? "I just don't think he should get all worked up about breaking some world record."

"Oh, I would never do that, Wart. Honest," said Bennie, looking very serious. "It's not good to break things. Right, Dad?"

Maya smiled at Bennie. "To break a record just means that one day you could be a faster puzzler than Deepika. Maybe it will be your name in the *Guinness World Records.*" Bennie sat up straighter. "But before that, you could start with entering our school talent show. That would be cool, wouldn't it?"

"Talent show? What's this about?" Mom asked as she placed a large plate of hot pancakes in the centre of the table.

Maya was wrecking everything and I was vibrating with anger. "Geez, it's nothing, Mom. Maya's got this crazy idea that Bennie should get up on the stage — in front of the whole school — and do one of his boring jigsaw puzzles. She doesn't get how that —"

"Yeah! I wanna do that." Bennie jumped off Dad's lap and strutted around the kitchen again. "I'm a puzzler. That's what puzzlers do — they do puzzles."

Maya clapped. My parents smiled. And Bennie danced.

"Here's a better idea, Maya. Why don't you do a puzzle in front of the whole school? How about that, eh? Oh, I can see it now. Everyone will flip over that, right, Maya?"

Bennie leaned in to my ear and cupped his hands. "I don't think that's a good idea at all, Wart. 'Member I told you, Maya's not so good at puzzles," he whispered.

"Well, if Bennie wants to do it, then I'll support him," said Mom. "And it would be nice if his brother did, too. Warren, how about it?" I didn't let her catch my eye.

Was I really the only one who knew how damaging something like this would be? Not only would Bennie look like a fool, though I doubted he'd care, but we'd both be made fun of for years. Since my parents seemed to be in the dark about how mean some kids could be, I was going to have to be the one to stop this train from leaving the station.

★ ⁂ ★

On Sunday afternoon the smells of Thanksgiving filled the house. Homemade pumpkin pie cooled on the stovetop, and a turkey roasted slowly in the oven. I loved Thanksgiving, but it would be our first without Gran and Granddad. Ever since Bennie and I were babies, we'd had all our special holidays with them.

At Thanksgiving, Gran always brought her famous ambrosia salad, full of pineapple, tiny oranges, and marshmallows — my favourite part of every holiday dinner. And Granddad always gave me a wink and said, "C'mon, sport, let's take a walk." We would go down to the river, where the banks were lined with maple trees in all the fall colours: orange and yellow and red. He liked to tell me stories about when he was a boy or when he first met my grandmother or when my dad was a kid. I loved having him to myself. To him I was the special one, not Bennie.

After I finished my homework, I was aching to get outside and slap the ball around. I went into the kitchen, where Dad was making his famous cheese and green bean casserole. "Hey, Dad, wanna play some hockey?"

"Sure. I'm just about finished here. Let's ask Mom and Bennie to join us."

I rummaged around in my closet for my extra sticks. Mom came into my room with some folded laundry. "Dad and I are going to play some hockey. Want to play, too?" I asked her.

"That sounds like fun. Afterward can I get you to peel the potatoes and carrots?"

"Sure. Where's Bennie?" I asked.

"He went over to Maya's house about an hour ago. He should come home anyway. I'm sure Maya's family is getting ready for their own Thanksgiving meal," Mom said.

"I'll get him." I ran out and jumped on my bike and rode past the empty lot, past Mrs. Smith's place and the Merchisons', and finally arrived at Maya's house. I knocked on her front door. When she answered, there were no yummy smells of turkey and pumpkin pie coming from her kitchen.

"I haven't seen him," she said when I asked about my brother.

"But my mom said he was coming here."

"Sorry. He's not here. Do you want me to help you look for him?"

Peering into the house, I said, "That's okay. He can't be too far. Maybe you can ask your brother if he's seen him."

"Taylor? He isn't here, either, and I don't know where he went."

At the end of Maya's driveway, I looked left and right, wondering where I should go next. Bennie didn't usually go too far from home. I rode my bike around the block, but didn't find him. So I crossed over Blundell Road and went as far as Williams, calling his name. Still nothing. By then my heart was starting to pound inside my chest. Bennie was super gullible, and I was always afraid some creep would lure him off with a jar of pickles and some peanut butter.

After checking all the obvious places, I couldn't decide if I should go home and get my parents or go just a little farther. I took a chance and rode to the corner grocer. Turning into the parking lot, I nearly slammed into a car pulling out. That's because standing out front of the busy store, with a cardboard sign around his neck, was my brother. His hair was messy, his face was dirty, and he had no shoes.

"Bennie!" I shouted, angry and relieved at the same time. "What are you doing?" Hopping off my bike, I read the sign around his neck and felt like a volcano was about to blow inside my brain. It said *I'm a pore liddle kid Give me monney.* I whipped the sign over his head and threw it onto the ground.

"Hi, Wart." Bennie beamed, happy to see me. "Look what I got." He held out a cup full of coins. Out of the corner of my eye I noticed a couple of heads bobbing over a hedge at the side of the entrance.

"Who … what … whose idea was it for you to beg for money? And … and where are your shoes?" I yelled.

A lady and her daughter stopped and dropped money into Bennie's cup. "Are you okay, sweetie?" the lady said to Bennie. She looked at me through squinty eyes. "Is this boy bothering you?"

"Nope. This is my brother, Wart. Can you give him some of your money, too?" Bennie asked her. Then he looked at me, smiling. "Afterward we can go and buy soda pop and candy, okay?"

The lady's face turned angry. "Disgusting! I thought this boy was in need." She grabbed her daughter's hand and marched back toward the door. "I'm going to tell the store manager about this." She turned and pointed her finger at me. "Using your brother to scam people — you should be ashamed of yourself!"

Just then Taylor and Luke came tearing around the corner on their bikes. They were pedalling pretty fast. "Taylor!" I yelled. He never looked back. "Did they put you up to this?" I asked my brother.

Bennie looked surprised. "You mad at me, Wart? Don't be mad. Look, I got lots of money. You can have it. Just gotta give the guys some, too."

The lady came back out of the store, followed by the manager. I grabbed my brother by the shirt. "Come on, we've got to get out of here." Bennie couldn't move very fast at the best of times, but without shoes it was nearly hopeless. "Seriously, where are your runners?" I shouted.

His eyes were big and round. "You're makin' me scared, Wart. What you so mad about?"

"Never mind." I growled at him like an angry dog. Then I started cussing as I tried to steer my bike with one hand and drag my brother with the other. "You're coming home with me."

"Wart," Bennie whimpered. "You're goin' too fast. And why ya so mad? We were just playin' a game."

I didn't talk to him all the way home. When we got to our house, Mom and Dad were talking over the fence with the neighbour, not a care in the world. I pushed Bennie toward them. "Here, he's all yours."

My mom looked like she was about to crawl out of her skin. "Warren!" she screeched. Then she looked at my brother. "Bennie? Why are you so dirty? And where are your shoes? Warren, what happened? What's this all about?"

I didn't bother to explain. "Ask him." I jumped back on my bike and rode like a demon over to Maya's house and pounded on the front door. She opened the door, a hot dog in her hand. "Hey, Warren. Did you find him?"

"Yeah, I found him," I roared. "Where's Taylor?"

"I don't know. He hasn't come home yet. You look really upset. What's the matter?"

"Ask your brother when you see him! And do me a favour — tell him I'm going to kick his butt when I find him." As I turned away, Maya's face was red, and her mouth, now filled with half-chewed hot dog, was gaping.

I took off, pedalling as fast as I could. I wasn't sure who I was madder at: Bennie, Taylor, or my parents. And this was their fault, so why was I the one feeling angry and embarrassed?

I rode around as the day faded into night and the street lights went on. A warm glow of light shone out of people's homes. I saw families gathered around their dining tables saying grace, telling jokes, maybe opening noisy crackers that had silly hats inside and tiny toys and sayings like "Be thankful for your family." *Blah blah blah!*

When the fury in my guts finally calmed down, I went home. By then the dining room table had been cleared and the good dishes, candles, and silverware put away. A single plate of food sat on the counter wrapped in plastic. Everyone was in the TV room, but I didn't go in to say hello. I popped the food into the microwave, and instantly the smell of turkey and gravy filled my nostrils, reminding me of the family dinner I'd missed. I went to my room to eat, but nothing tasted like it should.

CHAPTER 6

Monday was a holiday, so I stayed in bed late and thought about what to do about Bennie. Maya once said she sometimes pretended she didn't have a brother, especially when he acted like a fool. I decided that's what I would do.

From now on, the minute I left the house every day I would be Warren Osborne, only child. No more wondering or worrying about what people were thinking when they looked at Bennie. And I wouldn't try to find out what was happening to him, either, like if someone was tricking him into doing humiliating stuff. It would mean I wouldn't be so mad and uptight all the time. Best of all, I'd be responsible for no one but myself.

Dad poked his head into my room. "Warren, we're going to the pet store to get Jelly some cat food. Get dressed. We're leaving in ten minutes."

I loved going to the pet store and holding the rabbits and gerbils and feeding the budgies. "Who's going?" I asked.

"Just the usual suspects — Bennie and me."

This was the first test of whether I could stick to my new plan. Even though I really wanted to go, I wouldn't if Bennie was going. "Thanks, but not today, Dad. I'm tired."

"What? You're joking, right? You love going to the pet store."

I looked out the window so he couldn't see my face. I could see Owen's dad on a ladder, trimming some tree branches. I wondered if Owen was ever coming to school. So far he was like a fictional character or someone you can't prove exists, like Santa or God.

"Maybe next time. Besides, I've got homework to do," I lied.

"But it's our *thing*." I could tell Dad was surprised, maybe even disappointed. It bothered me, but not enough to make me change my mind. "If this is about yesterday —"

"It's not, Dad. I don't feel like going, that's all," I insisted. "But maybe one time just you and me could go to the pet store."

Dad looked like he wanted to say more, but he didn't. "Huh ... well, ah, sure, Warren."

The next day at school, I walked up to the class bulletin board, signed the volunteer chart, and sat down. Then I watched as the other kids arrived and added their names to the list, and to the one for the talent show. When Maya sat down in her seat next to mine, I looked away to the map on the opposite wall.

"I'm sorry about what Taylor did," she whispered at me.

"Sure," I said.

"You aren't mad at me, are you?" she asked. I didn't answer her. "That wouldn't be fair, if you were. I didn't know he'd do such a terrible thing."

"Not mad at you, Maya. Forget it." I opened my math notebook.

Mrs. Chapman called for our attention from the front of the room. "Okay, it looks like you've all signed up for a volunteering job. That's great. Some of you made some interesting choices." She looked right at me. "Nevertheless, these are all important contributions to the success of our school and student body. So, well done, class. There are still a couple of open spots if anyone wants to sign up for the talent show."

Mrs. Chapman then read out the list of who had volunteered for what. "Volunteers to help Miss Jones teach reading to her special needs students are Lily, Georgia, Ellen, Brett, and Maya. Volunteers for sweeping entryways are Timothy, Millie, and

Noreen. Schoolyard garbage cleanup are Nathan and Warren." She went on until she'd gone through the entire list.

For the rest of the morning, I avoided Maya. I knew she wanted to talk about what happened, but I didn't. And wouldn't.

When I got home from school, Mom was standing at the door. "Keep your coat on, kiddo. There's a sale on at Price Mart. We're going to get some new shoes for Bennie, and I thought we'd get you some of those sneakers you like, too. Since they're on half-price, we can even get you two pairs."

"That's okay. You and Bennie go. My old shoes are good enough," I said.

Her eyes went all big. "Well, this is a first. Warren Osborne turns down the chance to get new running shoes!" Then she became serious. "Okay, then, but don't come to me a month from now asking for new shoes. I'm not paying full price for something we could get on sale today."

"That's okay. I understand, Mom." I took my coat off and hung it in the hall closet. I could tell she didn't know what to make of me.

"We'll be a couple of hours. You'll be all alone," she said.

"I know." I went into the kitchen and poured myself a glass of milk.

"But you've never wanted to be at home alone before." Her voice got all screechy.

"I know, but now I do. I guess I'm growing up."

After a long silence she said, "Okay, fine." She grabbed Bennie by the hand. "Come on, honey. Apparently your brother doesn't need new shoes!" Just before closing the door, she said, "You don't go out anywhere, and keep the doors locked."

"Yes, Mom, I will."

Being alone was a new thing for me. I soon found out the house made noises I'd never noticed before. Like the gurgles from the plumbing, and the whistling of the wind sneaking through the cracks in the window frames. Worst was the furnace — it made me jump every time it started up. But it didn't take me long to get used to being alone. And I liked it.

* * *

Besides home, things became different at school. For one thing, I started playing hockey with the guys every day at recess and sometimes after school, too. I didn't exactly like Danny, or some of the other guys, but it was better than waiting around for some mysterious kid named Owen to show up and be my friend, or worse, having to play with nosy Maya.

"Where were you today?" Mom barked when I came home late one afternoon. Her face was redder than a fire truck and her voice shrill as a siren.

"What do you mean?" I said, bracing myself, though I really did know what she was talking about.

"I asked you this morning to get Bennie from his class after school and bring him to the parking lot and wait there for me. He had a dental appointment and I was short on time. Don't you remember?"

I did remember, but it just wasn't part of my plan. I pushed down the guilty feelings. "Sorry, I couldn't help it. I had to talk to Mrs. Chapman after school. She was helping me with fractions." Truth was, I'd been with the guys, playing hockey. I looked over at my brother, who was chewing on his fingernail. His cheeks were pink and he wouldn't look up from the floor. I think he knew I was lying. Never mind, I told myself. He'll get over it and so will she.

"Fortunately Maya found him wandering and took him to the front of the school and waited with him until I arrived," Mom said. "In the future I expect you to do as I ask, or at the very least call me if you're not able."

I stayed clear of Mom for the next few hours. She didn't get mad often, but when she did, it was best to give her space and time to cool down.

★　★　★

As the days passed, I got better and better at avoiding my brother outside our house. I was happy my plan was working, although it meant I didn't get to go out with my parents much. Still, I didn't have to look after Bennie anymore, and I didn't get angry or embarrassed, either. Some times were harder than others, like the afternoon when he showed up at my classroom. Mrs. Chapman called me to the cloakroom. Bennie was standing there, his head bent low and his arms crossed to hide the front of his pants.

"Looks like your brother could use your help," said Mrs. Chapman. He'd peed his pants and needed some spare clothes. The old Warren would have taken him to the bathroom and helped him change, but he would have been beet red in the face and mad about it, too. That's because as we walked to the bathroom there would have been kids in the hall staring and whispering and snickering, thinking I couldn't hear them. But the new Warren didn't have a brother who needed help.

"Sorry, I haven't got any spare clothes. He should just go to the office and call our mom. She'll come and look after him," I said, even though I really did have spares in my gym bag.

"He looks quite upset. Maybe you could talk to him and comfort him," said Mrs. Chapman.

I wasn't going to get sucked in. "He's fine. Right, Bennie? Just go to the office and call home. Mom will come." Then I went back to my desk and started writing in my notebook so I could avoid all the faces looking at me, including Maya's.

Mom did come, and like I thought, Bennie was fine. Proof that I didn't need to get involved and that Bennie didn't need me.

★　★　★

Before long, Halloween decorations started appearing everywhere. Mrs. Chapman had everyone in our class make posters to decorate the wall outside our classroom. I wasn't much for drawing or painting, but got the idea to make a big black pumpkin with orange eyes, nose, and mouth. Mrs. Chapman said she liked how I changed the colours of traditional pumpkin pictures. I think she said that because it's her job to be encouraging to every student, even the ones who are no good at art.

Unlike mine, Maya's was really good. I could tell she liked art because she put a lot of time into her poster. It had a spooky black tree against a bright yellow moon in the background, and sitting on the branches were a bunch of hunchback birds. At the bottom she wrote some words about fear in dripping red letters.

All around the school, kids talked about stuff like their costumes or who they were going trick-or-treating with. Then the list of performers for the talent show went up on the office bulletin board. I didn't have to check who was on it. I heard all about it from the guys.

"Another bunch of losers getting up to sing and dance," said Danny after school one day. "I even heard there's some stupid kid doing a puzzle. Can you believe it? Man, someone put me out of my misery now. Better yet —"

"Zip it, Danny. That's Warren's brother who's doing the puzzle," said Jesse.

I shrugged and gave a "don't worry about it" look. I was getting good at blocking any emotion when it came to Bennie.

"No. Tell me it isn't true, Wart. You going to let your brother do that? That's so lame. If he was my *twin* brother I'd — oh, but wait, he's not my *twin* brother. He's yours. Ha!" he said, smirking.

I amazed myself by brushing off his comment so easily. "Listen, Danny, I don't know anything about it, and I don't care." For some reason I really wanted him to believe it didn't bother me. "The whole talent show is a waste of time and I wish they'd cancel it."

When I got home that afternoon, Bennie was waiting at the door for me. "Hi, Wart. You gonna help with my costume? 'Cause I need one and Mom says I should ask you. That's 'cause you always have good ideas. Right?"

"I can't, Bennie. I don't have any good ideas this time. Ask Dad to help you. I bet he'll know what you can dress up as," I said as I headed for my room.

"But I want you to help me, Wart. You always help me." Bennie looked sad. Old Warren would have felt guilty and helped him. But the new one didn't have to feel responsible, didn't have to feel bad about stuff like that. It was time Mom and Dad looked after the little details in Bennie's life, not me.

That night Dad arrived home from work and flashed four tickets to that evening's hockey game. It was the Toronto Maple Leafs versus the Vancouver Canucks. At first I couldn't believe my luck. A live game — Leafs versus Canucks! But then I figured it out. This was just another trap.

"That's great. But Bennie doesn't even like hockey. Maybe he should stay home and I could bring one of the guys."

Dad went quiet, but not Mom. "Okay. That's enough of that, Warren. This is a family activity. That means your brother goes. Now, if you don't want to come — as it seems so often these days — then fine. But Bennie is going and that's final."

"Warren, we've tried to give you some space while you work through whatever it is you're needing to figure out. But it's gone too far now. We want our boy back," said Dad. "This is going to be fun. There will be eighteen thousand hockey fans cheering for the Canucks and only a small crowd cheering for the Leafs. We need you on our side, buddy."

He was making this really hard for me. But then I remembered the time we took Bennie to a game in Smiths Falls. He spilled his orange pop down the back of some guy sitting in front of us. The guy jumped up, looking like he was going to hammer Bennie. But when he saw that my brother had Down syndrome, he got all embarrassed and started apologizing instead. It would have been better if he'd just gotten mad. That would have been easier to deal with than his look of pity.

"Come on, son. You'll love it. You know you will," said Mom, now calmer.

I had to admit I was torn. It had been easy to give up the other outings, but this was different. I loved the Maple Leafs and it would be great to watch them take on the Canucks here in Vancover, in their very own rink. It would be even sweeter when they beat them. I could imagine the envy all over Danny's face when I told him I'd been there to see the whole thing live. But ...

"I would, but I promised Jesse I'd go to his house tonight and watch the game on TV. His dad just installed a home theatre and we get to be the first to try it out," I said. It was partly true — Jesse's family did get a new home theatre.

Dad scratched his head and looked at Mom. I could tell neither of them expected me to pass on something like this. "Well, if you really —"

"If Wart doesn't wanna go, can Maya come?" Bennie asked.

"Maya? Why should she get to go?" I blurted. It was hard enough passing up an opportunity like this, but to be replaced so easily — and by Maya — was insulting.

"Why should you care who we give the ticket to?" Mom asked. "Bennie, I'm fine with Maya coming. Go ask her."

Just like I thought, the Leafs beat the Canucks seven to five that night. And I wasn't there to see it.

Missing the game was pretty tough, but then, a week and a half before Halloween, something else happened. Something I didn't expect would bug me so much.

"Okay, ready, Bennie?" Mom asked as she pulled on her coat and grabbed her purse.

"Yup!" He already had his coat and hat on. He raced for the front door.

"Good," Mom said. "Bye, Warren. We'll see you later."

"What? Tonight's game night," I said, both surprised and annoyed.

"Sorry, Warren, not tonight," said Dad. "There's a special showing of the original *Ghostbusters* at SilverCity Cinemas. Best Halloween movie ever — and we're going to see it!" He pointed an imaginary ghostbuster ray gun and sprayed me with invisible slime.

I waited, expecting them to ask me to go with them, but instead Mom just said, "We should be home by nine o'clock. Lock the door after us."

What the heck? They not only didn't mention they were going to *Ghostbusters* until that very moment, but they didn't even bother to invite me. They knew how much I loved that movie.

I watched them leave and vowed to have a good time without them. First, I rummaged through every closet and cupboard until I found the bag of Halloween treats Mom had hidden. Then I flicked through all the TV channels to find a movie. I hoped one was playing *Ghostbusters*, even though I knew it wouldn't be as much fun as watching it on the big screen. Of course, it wasn't playing, so I settled for a dull old movie called *Shiver Me Timbers!* that wasn't even scary. After I'd stuffed my face with nearly the whole bag of little candy bars, I felt like barfing. If Mom knew, she'd say I deserved it.

I couldn't stop thinking about how mean my parents had been, though I vowed I wasn't going to let them know I was upset. That's why a few minutes before nine o'clock I shut off the TV and all the lights and went to bed. If they thought I was asleep I wouldn't have to talk to them when they came home.

I did a lot of tossing and turning before I finally drifted off to sleep. Sometime much later I felt something poking my arm. When I opened my eyes, I nearly jumped off the bed. Bennie stood over me, sniffling.

"Can I sleep with you, Wart?" he asked. Whenever Bennie got scared, he wanted to crawl into bed with me.

"We're too big to sleep together, Bennie. Go back to your own room," I grumbled.

"But I'm scared," he whimpered.

"Then get into bed with Mom and Dad." I turned over and covered my head with my blanket. But I could feel my brother staring down at me. I turned over and flung off the blanket. "Come on, you're going back to your own bed."

I took his hand and dragged him back to his bedroom. He didn't say a word.

"Here, now get into bed and stay there." The nightlight in the hall was bright enough to make the tears on my brother's face glisten. I felt annoyed at how they wormed their way into my heart. I let out a sigh and sat on the side of his bed. "What are you scared of, Bennie? Was there something in the movie that got to you?"

"No." He wiped his runny nose on the blanket.

Impatient and tired, I said, "Well then, what?"

Covering his eyes, he said, "I'm scared that I got no brains."

"What? Why'd you say that?" That came out louder than I'd wanted it to. I hoped I hadn't woken my parents.

"A boy at school said I got no brains. Said that's why I can't read and do other stuff. Is that true, Wart? Is it true I got no brains? 'Cause if it's true, that's bad, right?" He sniffled some more. "Mummies got no brains, either, do they? That's 'cause they're dead and someone sucked their brains out their nose. But I'm not dead, right, Wart? So how come I got no brains?" The tears were rolling down his cheeks now.

My body was a bundle of knots and I shook with anger. I tried to reassure him he was fine, but didn't know what else to say. I thought I'd gotten good at numbing out feelings about things people did or said to Bennie. But now, all I could think about was what I wanted to do to the jerk who told him he had no brains.

After a while Bennie got quiet, except for the sniffles. Then he said, "Wart, how come you don't like me no more?"

It felt like I'd just been kicked in the gut. "That's silly. I like you. Of course I like you. You're my brother."

"But you never want to go out with me." I could tell he was trying to study my face.

"I said I like you, Bennie."

"You do?" he said, sitting up. "Really? Not just sayin' that?"

"Yes, really." I smiled at him and patted his shoulder.

He leaped out of bed and threw his arms around my neck. "I'm sure glad, 'cause I was scared you didn't want me no more."

I peeled his arms off, tucked him in, and sat there on the side of his bed.

"Wart," he said sleepily, "will you help me with my Halloween costume?"

"We'll see," I said.

He yawned and then said, "Wart, you're the best brother in the whole world."

I sat there until I heard his heavy breathing turn into little snorts. Then I crawled back into my own bed, but it took me a really long time to fall asleep.

CHAPTER 7

"Mom, Mom, Mom," Bennie squealed when he came charging into the kitchen the next morning. "Guess what?"

"What?" Mom said, her eyes wide like she was ready to be amazed.

"Wart says he's gonna help me with my Halloween costume. Isn't that right, Wart?"

As I spooned cereal into my mouth, I could see the surprised look on Mom's face. "I said we'll see."

Bennie bounced over to the table like a kangaroo, and Mom put his toast down in front of him. "But you are, right? You're gonna help me make a Halloween costume, 'cause Halloween is coming real soon and Teacher says I got to have a costume for school. Isn't that right, Mom?" Mom smiled and nodded at him.

"So when you gonna help me, Wart?"

"Maybe when you stop calling me Wart."

Bennie put down his peanut butter and pickle toast. With a serious look on his face — well, as serious as you can get when your face is plastered in peanut butter and toast crumbs — he said, "Okay, I promise I won't call you Wart no more, even though that's your name. So what you want me to call you?"

"My real name, dufus."

"Dufus? That's not your real name." He scratched his chin, looking confused. "That's not his real name, right, Mom?"

Mom snickered from behind me. "You make a good point, Bennie."

"But I'll call you Dufus if that's what you want me to call you … Dufus." Bennie looked pleased with himself. I'd walked right into that one.

Mom covered her mouth, but I knew she was laughing. Then she got serious. "Thank you, Warren. I appreciate that you're going to help your brother. That means a lot to Dad and me."

I thought about the things Bennie had said the night before and wondered if she'd overheard. If she had, I was glad she didn't ask me about it.

★　✳　★

All that the kids talked about at school was the Halloween parade and talent show. They went on and on about it, whispering and giggling in class, at recess, and after school about their costumes and their acts and who would win the talent show prize.

Meanwhile, Bennie and I agreed we would dress up as pirates. His first choice was to be a zombie, but I hadn't forgotten what Taylor said, so I talked him out of it. It wasn't hard. He loved the movie *Pirates of the Caribbean*. We went to the dollar store and bought eye patches and a couple of tricorne hats, the kind of hats that looked like fancy triangles sailors wore in the old days. Mom said we could use her scarves for sashes, and she let us cut and tear pants and shirts we'd outgrown. Plus I found a recipe online for mangy beard stubble. Everything we needed was in the kitchen cupboard: flour, cornstarch, honey, and food colouring, plus a little water. After I made the stuff, I tested it out on Bennie. But he kept touching the goop before it dried, getting it in his hair and all over his shirt. In the end it looked like his chin was disintegrating — a good thing if you want to look like a zombie, but not so great if you want to look like an unshaven pirate. It was pretty funny, though, and Mom took a picture.

What wasn't funny was how Maya came over every day to coach Bennie on what he would do at the talent show. It was like she had decided she was his talent agent or something. The plan was for her to introduce him and his act, and then he would go up onstage and open the brand new jigsaw puzzle my parents had bought him for his demonstration. It was Maya's idea for him to do one he'd never done before. She said it would be more dramatic that way.

Worse than that, Maya got the principal, Mrs. Daniels, to agree that someone could film Bennie live as he put the puzzle together. He would be projected onto the big screen so the audience could watch as the puzzle took shape. Our music teacher, Mr. Carlton, even got in on the act. He was going to play suspenseful music on the piano, and just before Bennie finished, Chloe David would start to play a drum roll and then a final crash on the cymbals as he put the final piece in place.

"Videoing, music, drum rolls — none of that is going to make anyone want to sit around for fifteen minutes watching Bennie do a puzzle," I said. While I was secretly impressed about how many people were taking an interest, I yawned out loud to make my point.

"You need a nap, Wart?" Bennie asked.

"I'm not tired. I'm just imitating what all the kids are going to do if they have to sit and watch you do that puzzle."

Bennie squirmed excitedly. "But it's a really good one, Wart. See? Cupcakes! It's a yummy puzzle," he said and licked his lips. No wonder he'd been drooling on the box earlier.

"Sure it's nice, Bennie. But the kids are still going to be bored." I didn't want to hurt his feelings, but someone had to be honest with him.

"And that's where I come in," said Maya. "If you'd been listening, you'd know that Mrs. Daniels said acts had to be a maximum of five minutes. If we put my time and Bennie's together, that gives us ten minutes. He can easily put a hundred-and-fifty-piece jigsaw puzzle together in that amount of time."

"Let me get this straight. You're giving up your magic act so Bennie can have an extra five minutes to do his puzzle? How does that make things better, Maya?"

"No, silly. After Bennie gets started, I'm going to do my magic tricks — a sort of sideshow to his. Then when he's nearly done, Chloe will start to play the drum roll and we'll all watch him finish the puzzle. Good, eh?"

No, it wasn't good. The whole thing had turned into a circus and Bennie would be in the middle of it, like some kind of dancing bear or clown. And there was no point in talking to my parents anymore. They were just as excited as Bennie and Maya. They even booked off of work so they could be there to watch.

Neither of us would ever live this down. It was going to become one of those things people laughed about long after they'd all grown up. "I remember one time at school there was this kid …" they'd say.

And then they would drag up the whole story and laugh about it.

One thing was for sure. There was no way I would be able to watch it. I'd have to fake a stomach ache so I could stay home from school that day. Except it wouldn't really be faking, since I was pretty sure by the time the parade and talent show happened, my stomach would be tied up in knots for real. But staying home from school on Halloween day meant risking that I'd miss out on trick-or-treating that night. Mom always said if I was too sick to go to school, I was too sick to go out *after* school.

★ ★ ★

On the Saturday before Halloween, Maya was over — again — rehearsing the routine with my brother. He'd been doing a pile of puzzles that week, his way of getting in shape for the big performance.

"Wow, you did that one in eighteen minutes, Bennie. So if you can do a two-hundred-fifty-piece puzzle in that amount of time, then you should be able to do one hundred and fifty pieces in … let's see … fifty into two hundred and fifty equals five, and five divided into eighteen is …"

"Maya, you want a peanut butter and pickle sandwich? 'Cause I'm gonna have one," said Bennie.

"No, thanks," Maya said, trying to hang on to the mental math she'd been doing. "About three and a half minutes for every fifty pieces. Times that by three … that's a little more than ten and a half minutes to do a hundred-and-fifty-piece puzzle. We've got to find a way to cut that down by a minute, Bennie."

"You sure are good with numbers. Wish I could do that," Bennie said.

"Everyone is like that, Bennie. We all have things we're good at and things we wish we could do better. Take me for instance. I'm not good at puzzles."

Bennie's head popped up and he laughed. "That's for sure!" Then he clapped his hand over his mouth. "Oops. Sorry, Maya. I shouldn't say that. It's not nice to say things like that. Right, Wart?"

I chuckled, and Maya gave me the evil eye but smiled at Bennie. "That's okay. I forgive you, Bennie. Like I said, we all have things we're good at, and others we're not. Take your brother — he's pretty good at hockey, but doesn't have any manners."

"*Ouch!* That hurt," I said, pulling a pretend arrow out of my heart. Bennie giggled. He always laughed at my jokes.

Maya ignored me. "Bennie, I've been wondering. Why are jigsaw puzzles so easy for you?" It was a good question. I don't think anyone had ever asked him that before.

Bennie held his new puzzle box and traced the picture on the top with his finger. He looked up and smiled. "It's not so hard, Maya. I have this picture on the box to look at. See?" He held up the picture of rows of cupcakes decorated with icing and candy. He smacked his lips.

"Yeah, but once the picture is broken into tiny pieces, all those bits look the same," she said.

Bennie looked surprised. "The same? That's not true, Maya. They don't look the same at all." He picked up some of the pieces from the puzzle on the floor. "See? Every piece got its own shape and colour. They're all different, just as different as red and yellow, or me and Wart. Oops, sorry, Dufus. Didn't mean to call you that."

Mom came into the room snorting like a hog, and a flash of heat burned across my cheeks. When she finally stopped laughing, she noticed Maya looking confused. "Just a little family joke, Maya. And Bennie, I think your brother would rather you call him Warren. Okay?"

Bennie shrugged agreeably. "I don't mind, but it was his idea to call him Dufus."

"Well, let's just stick to Warren, okay? Now please go on and finish what you were saying. I'm curious, too, about why you find puzzles easy."

Bennie scratched his head, like he'd forgotten what he was saying.

"You said puzzles are easy because you can see how each piece is different," I reminded him. "As different as you and me."

"Right, different as you and me. But even if they're all different, they're part of the same picture. So that's why I gotta start with the whole picture first, 'cause that reminds me how every piece has only one place it can go. Get it?"

"Not really," Maya said.

Bennie had this thing he did when he was thinking hard. He'd make this yoga kind of pose with his legs bent open, his feet pressed together sole to sole, and his knees touching the floor as if his legs were rubber bands. Then he'd bend over and put his elbows on the floor and rest his head on his hands, which made him look like a human pretzel. He sat like that for a bit, then suddenly looked over at our family portrait on the wall.

"Warren is like a puzzle piece. There's no other one like him in the whole world. And we need him — Mom and Dad and Jelly and me — to make our puzzle perfect," said Bennie. I didn't know why, but I had a sudden urge to hug my brother.

"It's the same for you, too, Maya. There's no other puzzle piece just like you. And your dad and Taylor and Warren and me, we gotta have you to finish our puzzle picture. Nobody else can fit in this place 'cept you. See? And it's not hard to know where you belong, 'cause there's only one spot that's shaped like you. Guess that's how come I can do puzzles easy. I see how every piece is different and how only one piece can fit into one spot. That's 'cause each one is like no other piece. And when each piece is in its right place, the picture looks perfect — just like the one on this box."

Maya sighed. "So are you saying that to you, each puzzle piece is like looking at the face of someone in your life, like the whole world is one big puzzle picture?"

He nodded.

"That's cool, Bennie. I think you're amazing."

Bennie wrinkled his nose and smiled. "That's what Mom always says, too. Right, Mom? You always say, 'Bennie, you're amazing. You're one of a kind.'"

"You're right. That's what I always say, sweetie." Mom's cheeks were glowing pink. "You're one of a kind."

"But, Mom, that's true about Maya, too, right?"

Mom nodded.

"And Duf ... Warren?"

Again she nodded.

"It's true about everyone?"

Mom nodded one last time. Bennie was quiet for a while and then said, "Yup, we're all amazing. We're all like pieces in a super-duper big jigsaw puzzle. Right, Mom?"

Mom pulled Bennie onto her knee. "I think you've put it exactly right, son."

"Mom?"

"Yes, Bennie?"

"I'm hungry. Can I have toast with peanut butter and pickles now?" Pretty soon we were all splitting our guts with laughter.

Sometimes I was frustrated or embarrassed by my brother. But he was right, there was no other piece in the puzzle like him, and I was glad he was in my family. I liked that he was always nice to people, even those who weren't nice back. And he didn't worry about what people thought of him, either. But even better — and the thing I liked best about him — was that he was always happy. Not because life was easy for him. It wasn't. It's just that even when things were hard he could always see the bright side.

When we were little, I learned to walk a long time before Bennie did. Mom said she worried that he'd never walk. Then one day when we were three years old, we were at my grandparents' house. There was a bowl of strawberries on the table, and I walked over and ate some. I guess Bennie wanted some, too, but nobody noticed. Out of the blue, he got up all on his own and took his first wobbly steps toward those berries. Funny thing about that was how Mom just cried and cried. That's how happy she was.

I sure don't remember her ever crying like that over something I learned to do.

After that, it was still a long time before Bennie could walk well on his own, and even longer before he learned to run. By then I was already pretty good with a soccer ball and a hockey stick.

Learning to talk was just as hard for him. That's because his pudgy tongue always got in the way and he sounded as though his mouth was full of marshmallows. A lot of time with the speech therapist helped to fix that — mostly.

When we turned six, things finally started to get easier for Bennie. And that's also when he discovered puzzles. For some reason, a mystery even the doctors couldn't explain, puzzles were as easy for him as running and kicking a ball were for me.

Along the way, I suppose I'd gotten used to seeing him doing puzzles and forgot that it was something special. That he was special. Not my parents — they never forgot to celebrate every new thing he learned to do.

But there were some things that I hadn't forgotten. Like when Bennie was learning to do things on his own, I learned that some people weren't comfortable around him. While my parents were just proud and happy he could finally walk and talk, strangers only saw that his flat feet made him slow and unsteady and that his fat tongue didn't fit his mouth and made it hard to understand his words. And that compared to me, he was small and acted younger.

At the parks, some moms moved their babies away when Bennie came to play. I don't know why exactly. Maybe they thought Down syndrome was like a disease you could catch. And kids laughed when he stumbled or dropped things or blurted out silly words that made no sense. Bennie never seemed to notice the looks, but I did. To him, everyone in the world was his friend.

Then one day a boy came up to him on the playground and said, "You a retard?" I watched my mom. She stood there, her mouth hanging open. Then I saw she had tears in her eyes so I socked the kid.

Back in Smiths Falls, my best friends were used to Bennie. They never asked me useless things like "What's wrong with him?" or "Will he always be that way?" or "Is there a cure?" Sure, they knew he wasn't like everyone else, but at least they accepted him. Then we moved, and ever since then it was like I didn't know how to be anymore.

Everyone says that being twins is something really special and that Bennie and I are even more special — like one in a million. So why did I feel like I'd been robbed? Sure, I had a brother, and a really nice one, but he would never be someone I could tell all my secrets or fears to, or ask for help in solving a problem. And I never felt like we were connected the way brothers are supposed to be. It had always been so confusing. I wanted people to accept him as he was, but at the same time, I wished he were *normal* and that we could just be like regular brothers.

But that's not how it was, and it never would be. In my world, everything was about Bennie, for Bennie, because of Bennie. Would it be so wrong if, for once, things were the way I wanted them to be? All I wanted was for my brother and me to be free of snooping and judging eyes. But that was never going to happen if he did the talent show. Instead we'd both look foolish.

So I had no choice. I needed to stop him from going onstage and making a fool of himself — and me. Maybe I didn't know how to stop Bennie, but I was pretty sure I knew someone who did.

CHAPTER 8

After ball hockey that Sunday afternoon, I brought up the topic of the talent show with the guys.

"So let me get this straight. You want me and the guys to help you come up with a plan to stop your brother from being in the talent show?" said Danny, grinning. When he said it out loud like that, he made it sound diabolical. "Why would I want to do that to Bennie? I was kind of looking forward to watching the little dude put a puzzle together. Right, guys?" He snored loudly and most of the boys sniggered. Not Cam. Not Jesse, either — he looked worried.

"Look, I don't want to be a part of this," said Jesse. He grabbed his stick and jacket. "See you tomorrow."

"Hey, wuss, keep your mouth shut," warned Danny as Jesse rode off on his bike. I swallowed hard, wishing I could ride off, too. But then Danny stepped closer. "Like I said, Wart, what's in it for me?"

"Ah, well … how about the satisfaction of helping a friend? Of helping to keep my brother from becoming the butt of everyone's jokes?" As the words spilled out of my mouth, I realized how dumb they must have sounded to someone like Danny. "You know what? Forget it. It was a crazy idea."

"You can't wimp out now," Danny said, gripping my arm. "And why save just your brother? Why not put an end to the whole mind-numbing talent show? Save all those freaks from making fools of themselves."

Jeff, David, and Andy hooted and gave each other high fives.

Cam looked nervous. "Ah, hey, guys, I got to go home. My mom wants me to chop firewood." He tore off.

"So, how are we going to do this thing?" said Danny. "It's got to be the prank of the century."

"We could pull the fire alarm just as everyone gets seated in the gym," said David, stomping his foot. "That would be so funny, seeing everyone running around like chickens with their heads cut off."

"Yeah, it would be funny. But do you think they send kids to jail for stuff like that?" asked Jeff. David stopped laughing.

"Better not risk it," said Andy. "How about we put glue all over the chairs? That would be even more hilarious. Can you picture everyone trying to get up?"

Danny shook his head in disgust. "You guys are so lame. This prank has to be so awesome that it deserves to win the talent show prize. It's got to be so good it clears the room *and* makes all those idiots freak out."

The guys squirmed happily over this, but I was hung up on the word *idiot*. Who was he talking about?

"What's the matter, Wart? You look all uptight. Don't worry. Leave it to me to come up with a plan. But we'll need to act fast since the talent show is next Friday," he said. "And remember, this is a secret, so not a word to anyone. Not to Cam, and especially not to Jesse." He pointed a finger at me. "You got it? Not a word."

* * *

Monday morning, Danny was standing on the front steps of the school. As Andy, Jeff, and David passed him, he handed them each a slip of paper. He handed me one, too.

"We're making stink bombs, lots of stink bombs," he whispered. "Everyone brings one ingredient. That way parents won't get suspicious. We're meeting at four o'clock at Greenway Park."

When I got to my classroom, I quickly opened the note. It read *one jar of peanut butter*. Oh, man! Why did it have to be peanut butter?

I took my seat and tried to ignore the hard lump inside my guts. It was telling me that if this thing didn't work, I had a lot to lose. For starters, if we got caught, I'd probably get suspended from school and be lumped in with the bad kids forever. And there was no saying what my parents would do. Then again, if the plan succeeded, it might be even worse. I would be forever in Danny's debt.

I rubbed my aching head. This thing I'd started was beginning to feel like a train slowly speeding up. Before long there'd be nothing to stop it, nothing except a train crash — and that wouldn't be pretty.

When I passed the guys in the hall at recess, they all smiled deviously and stuck their hands out to give me a high five. Jesse saw us. I knew because he looked right at me. A wave of guilt washed over me and left beads of sweat all over my forehead. Luckily, Nathan and I had garbage duty at lunch, and he always talked so much I never had time to think.

As soon as the last bell went that afternoon, I whipped home before Maya had a chance to corner me. Luckily, I got there before Mom and Bennie. I opened the pantry and found the last jar of peanut butter on the shelf. There was a third of a jar left in the fridge, so I figured I should be good at least for a day or two, but it wouldn't be long before Mom or Dad discovered that we were out of peanut butter. With luck Mom would think it was Bennie who had eaten it up, because she never got mad at him.

I glanced at the clock and saw that I didn't have time to worry about it. I stuffed the jar in my backpack and raced to Greenway Park on my bike. The guys were hanging out at the edge of the woods, just behind the bathrooms, the perfect place for making something stinky.

"Finally, it's odd Osborne. Thought maybe you were going to chicken out," said Danny.

The smirk on his face made my legs twitch, like they had a mind of their own and wanted nothing more than to kick him. But I couldn't afford to do that — not now.

"Okay, everybody, let's see what you've got," said Danny.

Jeff opened a carton of brown eggs and placed them gently on the ground. David put down his jug of milk. And Andy pulled a big bottle of vinegar out of his backpack and some Ziploc bags. Finally, I added my jar of peanut butter.

Danny picked it up. "Nice, chunky style. That'll make it look especially disgusting." A couple of the guys laughed nervously.

"You sure this is going to work?" asked David. "Bet Owen's got some super-toxic concoction. We should ask him."

"Shut up, dork!" said Danny. "You think I'm stupid? I got this recipe off the internet." Then he spat out, "Owen! We don't need him. And for that matter, we don't need you, either."

David's cheeks turned pink and he seemed to get real small.

"So, we going to do this, or not?" asked Danny.

The boys came in closer as Danny set out a large mixing bowl, the only thing he'd brought. David poured in his milk, while the rest of us cracked eggs and dumped them — shells and all — into the bowl. Danny picked up a stick and stirred until the yolk floated in little yellow swirls on the surface, looking as harmless as Mom's omelettes.

I was thinking about what David had said about Owen having a good concoction. It made me wonder if he was the kind of guy who would want to be a part of our plan to ruin a favourite school tradition. If he was, would he be the kind of person I would want for a friend? As I looked around at the guys and thought about what we were doing, I realized maybe I wasn't the kind of guy that he'd want to know.

"Okay, dump in the vinegar, Andy." Danny handed me the stick. "And you, time for the final touch."

I scooped the peanut butter into the mixture and stirred. Andy started gagging. "Oh gawd, I don't think I'll ever be able to eat peanut butter again," he said.

Looking down at what now looked like a curdling swirl of runny baby poo — and would soon smell like it, too — I knew there was no way I'd ever be able to look at peanut butter the same way, let alone eat it. While Andy hurled into the trees, the rest of us chuckled uncomfortably. I think it was because we knew it wouldn't take much for us all to be doing the same.

"Who's going to pour it into the bags?" asked David. "'Cause I'm not." Everyone echoed his refusal.

"Well, it's gotta be you then, Wart. This whole thing is because of you," said Danny, grinning. Holding his nose, he pushed the bowl closer.

"Me? You're the one who came up with the idea to make stink bombs." I looked down at the chunky brown mixture in the bowl and my stomach gurgled and heaved. The boys crowed. They knew I was stuck with the job — and so did I. "Fine, I'll do it, but you're holding the bags!" I shoved them toward Danny.

"All right, but you get any of that crap on me, and I'm going to soak your head in it," he warned. And I knew he would, too.

"Come on. Let's get this over with." I took a deep gulp of air and was glad I was good at holding my breath. The guys choked, hooted, gagged, and yelled the whole time until the bowl was empty.

"Now that that's over, who wants to take this stuff home?" said Danny. No surprise he didn't get a volunteer. "Jeff, you do it."

Jeff's eyes popped. "Not me. My dog, Jack, is a German shorthaired pointer. They use dogs like him to sniff out bombs and drugs. He'll find this stuff in no time and tear open the bag. My mother will kill me."

David said, "Tough. There are five bags and five of us. I say we each take one stink bomb. That's fair."

"Good idea," said Danny before Jeff could object. "You gotta find the hottest place in your house. Heat is the final ingredient. Helps this stuff rot faster and get good and stinky. I'm going to put mine right on top of the water heater. Nobody will notice it there."

"So what's the rest of the plan, Danny? Where we putting the stink bombs on the day of the talent show?" Andy asked.

"Let's save one for Mrs. Daniels's office. She told my mom I'm late for school all the time. Now I gotta get up half an hour earlier every morning," complained David.

"Not happening," said Danny. "But the rest of the plan is pretty straightforward. After the Halloween parade, we'll walk into the school with the rest of the kids. I'll be up at the front. You guys will spread out in the middle and in the back as everyone piles into the gym for the talent show. When I give the signal, we'll quietly drop these stinky babies on the floor and keep walking. They'll pop open when kids step on them. And once they start to get a whiff, they'll be running around trying to get away. It'll be chaos. Ha!"

"Eww," groaned Andy, cupping his mouth. "Does that mean it's going to be all over our shoes?"

"Not if you go over to the side of the gym. And trust me, these things are going to stink so nasty and look so disgusting, there'll be kids running around yelling and barfing everywhere." Danny was cracking up hysterically. "It won't take long to clear the whole school. And while there's chaos and they're all getting tortured, we just slip out unnoticed. It'll be awesome. It'll be the best prank ever."

We loaded the stink bombs into our backpacks and rode home. Every time I hit a bump or a pothole, I cringed. I had no idea how strong those plastic bags were and didn't want to find out. When I got into the house, Bennie was sitting in the kitchen, licking his fingers. I nearly gasped. He'd just about polished off the last of the peanut butter from the fridge.

"Hi, Wart. Where ya been?" he asked.

"Nowhere. Hey, Bennie, you better take it easy on the peanut butter. You eat too much of that stuff," I said.

He looked at me like I was as nutty as his peanut butter and shook his head. "Mom says peanut butter is protein. Protein's good for you, don't you know?"

★   ★   ★

The next morning, Maya surprised me from behind. "Hi, Warren." I jumped at the sound of my name, and she laughed. "You're kind of jumpy, aren't you?" she said.

I shook my head and shrugged.

"No? Well, if you say so. Hey, there's something I want to talk to you about. Can we meet at recess?" Then she added, "I know, it's hockey time, but just this once, could we hang out instead?"

I didn't want to play with the guys at recess anyway. "I guess. What's it about?" I wondered if Jesse or Cam blabbed about the plan to ruin the talent show.

"All right, class. Time to get to work," said Mrs. Chapman.

Maya sat down at her desk and whispered, "We'll talk at recess, okay?"

Maya was right. I was jumpy. Ever since I'd got Danny involved, I was definitely feeling nervous. More than ever I wished I had someone to talk to, like Granddad or my old friend, Michael Jeffers. I knew there was no point in talking to my parents. They were too busy — mostly making life better for Bennie.

The morning dragged on, and was about as exciting as watching grapes turn into raisins. Nothing Mrs. Chapman said stuck in my head, and I hoped she wouldn't ask me a question. When the bell finally rang, I was the first one to the door and down the hall. I waited for Maya by the soccer field.

"Boy, you sure were in a rush. What's the matter? Spelling rules not your favourite topic?" Maya said, grinning.

"Oh, is that what we were learning?"

"Kidder." Maya bumped me on the arm.

"So, what did you want to talk about?" I asked, a little afraid of what she was going to say.

Maya pulled me to the side and started talking in a low voice. "It's about the talent show."

Shoot! "Look, I don't know what Jesse told you, but I'm —"

"Jesse? He didn't tell me anything. Why? What's he up to?" Her eyes were narrow and she looked suspicious.

So he hadn't talked to her. I had to backtrack quickly. I laughed and said, "Oh, he's just looking forward to the talent show is all … wanted me to tell him what tricks you're going to do."

Maya looked at me like I was a cracked egg. "You didn't tell him, right? Better not have."

I zipped my lips and mumbled, "Not a word."

"Okay, good. Besides, I've got something way more exciting to tell you. But it's a secret, so you've got to promise not to tell." I waited for her to go on. "Well? Are you going to promise?"

"Sure, I promise. What's the secret?"

"I'm not sure that sounded like a real promise," Maya said impatiently.

"Maya." I said her name real slow so I'd sound more sincere. "I promise I won't tell anyone your secret. There, is that good enough?"

She kicked at the pebbles on the ground and grinned. She liked to do that, drag out her stories, or secrets, and make me wait. Finally, she said, "There's going to be a surprise act in the talent show, and I know who it is."

"Yeah?" I said aloud, but I was thinking, *There isn't going to be a talent show for this surprise act.*

She looked from side to side, as if making sure no one else could hear. Then she whispered, "It's Owen." I didn't respond, so she said it again. "Warren, did you hear me? It's Owen."

"But ... but the deadline is past. It's too late for any new acts. Mrs. Daniels said so." I didn't know if my face looked odd, but it sure felt funny. Like maybe all the blood had drained away.

"I know, right? But she gave him special permission. I think it was real nice of her. And you'll flip out when you hear what he's doing for his act."

"But ... but you said he was still feeling self-conscious about the way he looks. That he wasn't ready for everyone to see him," I said weakly.

"I thought you'd be excited about this." Maya crossed her arms and shot darts at me with her eyes.

"No, I am. I'm excited." I gave her a little smile, hoping it looked real. "It's just I'm surprised that his first time back is going to be getting up in front of the whole school. Won't that be hard?"

"Yeah, it'll be really hard for him to get onstage. He didn't want to at first, but I convinced him and his mom that this would be the perfect time. Let everyone have a good look at him and get over all the weirdness, and then hit them with his big surprise. Everyone will be so amazed they won't even be interested in what he looks like anymore."

I was suddenly really mad. "Isn't it enough that you got Bennie up there doing a ridiculous puzzle? Now you've got Owen, too. What's he going to do, tap dance?"

"Don't be a jerk, Warren."

Okay, I admit what I said was mean, but I was upset about what she'd just told me.

Maya's frown turned to a smug grin and she said, "For your information, he and his dad built a robot."

"Yeah, Bennie told me," I mumbled.

"But did he tell you that it can juggle?" I guess the look on my face said it all. "Ha! Didn't think so." Maya started to laugh. "This is going to be the coolest talent show ever."

"Yeah. Real cool," I said. Suddenly my mouth was very dry and my knees felt weak.

CHAPTER 9

After school I walked to my bike in a daze. I didn't know what to do with this new information about Owen. The plan to stop the talent show wasn't just at home in a bag, turning into a slimy, stinking monster. It was in my head, festering into a giant guilt trip.

As I was getting on my bike, someone behind me shouted, "Wart! Wait up." Danny came over like a brewing storm, his fists clenched and eyes beady. "You won't believe what happened. Last night David's baby sister found his stink bomb and opened it. The dipstick left it behind her toy box. She smeared it all over herself and her bedroom."

"Oh, that's bad. Really bad!" My guts squirmed just thinking about that gunk covering his sister from head to toe. Apart from the horrid smell, she must have looked like a real live poo emoji. "What did he tell his mom?"

"She freaked. She thought the baby was having a major case of diarrhea and rushed her off to the hospital. Thanks to David, we're now down a stink bomb. I knew he couldn't handle it. Should've never let him be in on our prank." Danny kicked at the chain-link fence. "At least he didn't tell his mom what it really was, so the plan is still on."

⭐ ⭐ ⭐

I had a hard time concentrating on homework that night. Dad checked my math problems and they were all wrong. "What's gotten into your head, buddy?" he asked. "Something on your mind?"

Boy, that was an understatement. As if ruining the talent show wasn't enough, now I had David's baby sister and Owen to feel bad about. "Nope," I said, trying to sound chirpy. "I'm fine." I don't think he believed me.

"Well, maybe you're just tired. Why don't you head off to bed? You can finish this in the morning."

"Yeah. Think that's what I'll do. Good night, Dad."

Before crawling into bed I checked on my own stink bomb. I'd tucked it behind my laundry basket, which was directly in front of the radiator in my room. I knew heat was important for turning what would otherwise be a gross but harmless omelette into a disgusting air killer. When I'd put it there, I'd thought it was the best place, but after hearing what happened to David's bomb, I wondered if I should have hidden it behind the furnace in the basement.

I picked it up and gave it a good shake. As I was setting it back down on its opposite side, Jelly came and brushed up against me. I pushed her away, and she flicked her tail at me, annoyed that I hadn't patted her. Remembering David's baby sister, I imagined her using her claws to tear open the bag out of spite. Just the thought of that brown crud leaking onto my bedroom carpet, getting on my clothes, and filling the air gave me shivers. I quickly covered the stink bomb with an empty shoebox I'd been using to hold some of my hockey cards, satisfied it would keep the bomb safe from her.

A moment later, Mom knocked on my bedroom door. "Warren, can I come in?" She was carrying a glass of milk and a huge chocolate-chip oatmeal cookie. "Here, I thought you might like a snack before bed." As I munched on it quietly, I could tell she was studying me carefully. "Dad said you seemed a little off this evening. What's going on? Everything okay?"

"Yup, I'm good." I crawled under my quilt and nibbled some more at my cookie. I hoped she would leave, but she hovered over me.

"You excited about Halloween?" she asked. She sat down on the edge of my bed. *Nuts!* I was cornered now. The thing about Mom was she could sniff out trouble better than a hound dog. So I had to choose my words carefully.

"Uh-huh," I mumbled, washing down the last bite of cookie with milk.

"Got everything ready for the parade?"

"Yeah." I yawned and rubbed my eyes. *Hint, hint, Mom.*

"Looking forward to it?" I shrugged so I didn't have to lie. But then she just sat there and stared at me hard.

Man! Usually when I wanted a little of her attention, she was busy — mostly because of something she was doing for Bennie. But now, when I just wanted to be invisible, she was all over me. The last thing I needed or wanted right now was one of her talks.

"It's fine, Mom. I'm just tired." I did my best to look stoked. "It's going to be great!" The minute I said it I knew I'd made the mistake of saying the word *great* like Tony the Tiger: *GRRREAT!*

She just sat staring at me until I broke under the pressure.

"Okay. So I'm not excited. I hate parading around in front of other people. You know I don't like being watched."

"You don't like being watched? Or you don't like Bennie being watched?" Mom asked.

"Both. Now can I go to sleep?" I pulled the covers up to my chin, hoping she'd get the point.

"Warren, this has got to stop. You're trying way too hard to be in control — of Bennie and of what people think of him, and of you. You can't control all those variables. You can only control how you want to be in this world."

I knew she would say something like that. "Why can't you get it, Mom? I'm not like you."

She sat quietly. I could tell she was thinking. Then she said, "And what about the talent show? I guess you're still worried about that, too, about what the kids are going to think or do when they see Bennie doing his puzzle."

I wanted to say, *Actually, Mom, right now I'm more worried about getting caught letting off stink bombs in the school and getting suspended. I'm more worried about ruining my chances of having good friends, like Jesse and Owen, and even Maya. I'm worried I'll spend the rest of my life being the son who disappointed his parents and screwed up his brother's chance to show the one super-cool thing he could do.* In the end, all I said was, "It'd be easier if he didn't do it."

"You might think I don't understand how you're feeling, but honey, I understand only too well." Mom went over and closed my bedroom door and came back to sit on the end of my bed.

"Mom, I'm too tired for this. Can't we have this talk tomorrow?" I said with as much annoying whine in my voice as I could muster. But she ignored it.

"Warren, I've never told you about the day you and Bennie were born. It was the most terrifying and most exciting day of my life. We knew we were having twins. First, you came out and the doctor gave us a hearty congratulations. Then a few minutes later, Bennie was born. Only this time, the doctor was quiet. When he didn't say, 'Wow, congratulations, you're the proud parents of another baby boy,' I instantly got scared. He looked at me sadly and said, 'I'm sorry, Mrs. Osborne, but it looks like your second baby boy has Down syndrome. It's unusual enough just having identical twins, but then for one to have Down syndrome, too, is quite an anomaly.'

"Here was what should have been Bennie's welcome into the world with joy and celebration, but instead he was presented more as a disappointing anomaly. He wasn't even a minute old and he'd already failed as a human being. Well, you can imagine, having just given birth to two babies and hearing the doctor's comments, I started to cry. I guess he mistook my tears for grief, because the next thing I knew, they sent in a social worker to comfort me. She suggested that Dad and I had 'options' — like placing Bennie in foster care."

"What? She really said that?" At first I was shocked, but then guilt squeezed at my guts and my heart when I remembered how I had pretended I had no brother, no Bennie in my life. Just the thought that it could actually have been true scared me and filled me with dread.

"Yes, she really said that. Of course, we never considered it, not even for a moment. How could we? We had two beautiful boys and they belonged to us and we were taking them home." Mom sighed heavily.

"But it didn't end there, Warren. Once we got home, there were all the pitiful looks from relatives and friends. Not from Gran and Granddad, though, bless their hearts, never from them. I just hated those looks of pity from others. 'Oh, you poor thing. How sad it is your baby has Down syndrome.' Then they'd look at you and say, 'At least you have Warren.'"

My cheeks were suddenly hot and my guts felt all twisted inside me.

"But the fact is, I'm not some poor thing. Bennie is a light in my life. He's joyous and innocent and gentle and he loves everyone. He's fearless and there's no one he wouldn't do a kindness for." Mom leaned closer and looked me in the eyes. "And there's no one he cares more about than his wonderful brother. He idolizes you, and you know it."

Mom went on. "Early on I realized I had a decision to make, Warren. I could let those people who stared and pitied us bother me, or I could say, 'Forget it,' and let you and Bennie fill my soul with your goodness instead." She dabbed at her eyes, and I reached out and took her hand. "So you see, honey, I get where you're coming from. I really do. But along the way, I decided not to care about what others were thinking or saying. I hope one day you'll come to that same conclusion."

I was feeling bad before, but now I could hardly breathe for fear I'd start to cry. I thought about all the times my family had gone to the movies or to parks or to shopping malls. I always wondered why my parents never noticed when some lady did a double take at Bennie and then looked so sad. Or why they never heard the little remarks by old folks who looked at him like he was some kind of extraterrestrial. I thought I was the only one who noticed those things. Now I saw it wasn't that they didn't notice or care. They chose not to notice or care.

How easy life would be if I could be like that. To just be Bennie's brother, without any expectation, without a care about what went on in other people's minds.

Just then, Dad popped into the room. "Honey, sorry to disturb you and Warren, but I'm trying to make Bennie's lunch for tomorrow. I thought we had a new jar of peanut butter, but I can't seem to find it anywhere. And you know what he'll be like if he doesn't get his fix of PB."

"Don't worry, it's there somewhere. I'll be out in a minute to help you look for it," said Mom.

My heart suddenly went into overdrive. I was pretty sure my face went pale, too, so I covered it with my hands and yawned loudly. "Think I need to go to sleep now."

"Are you sure there isn't something else on your mind? Because no matter what, I want to make sure you've had a chance to say whatever you want or need to."

I shook my head and turned over to face the wall. "No, I'm good. Just really tired."

"Okay, son. Have a good sleep." She turned off the light and left.

Fact was, I really was tired. Tired of lying. Tired of the awful and mean plan to ruin the talent show. Tired of always wanting to be cool, but never quite making it; of always being angry with people who were weird around my brother. Tired of wishing for a best friend. And now, to top it off, Bennie wasn't going to get peanut butter for lunch tomorrow.

During the night, I had so many weird dreams. In one, Bennie got swallowed up in a giant vat of peanut butter. In another, I was forced to stand on the stage at school in my underwear blowing "Jingle Bells" on my armpits — and no one laughed.

★   ★   ★

I spent most of Wednesday avoiding the guys. I didn't feel so much like playing hockey or hanging out. But Thursday morning, Danny was waiting for me at the footbridge on the way to school. "We need to talk. Got some more bad news," he said. Andy was with him, but not Jeff or David.

I dropped my bike on the grass.

Danny blurted, "Jeff weaseled out."

"What do you mean?" I said, fear trundling up from my guts. "Did he tell on us?"

"No. The dummy bailed on us. He chickened out. That's what I mean. After what happened to David's sister — I don't know, he just lost his nerve. Gutless twit." I could see the muscles on Danny's neck twitching. "So it's just the three of us now. You, Andy, and me gotta carry this thing off."

"Do you think we can trust him? Who's to say he won't tell on us?" said Andy.

Danny punched him hard in the arm. "He won't tell. Trust me!" he said. Andy rubbed his arm and looked tense.

At first I was a little stunned to hear that Jeff backed out. But then it dawned on me: this was my way out, too. In my heart I never really wanted to go through with the prank and ruin the talent show. Mom had me pegged right. I had to stop being so hung up about what the kids at school thought about Bennie or me. And even if his performance was boring or the kids laughed at him, I could live with that, because, I realized, I cared more about *him* than them.

"You know, Danny, I think this is a sign that we should drop the plan. Let the kids have their talent show," I said. "And besides, it's Halloween. We'll find some wicked cool way to use our stink bombs." I watched how his eyes got small and his jaw started to grind.

"That's lame, Wart. You're just as much of a coward as Jeff. And all this time I thought *you* were the twin with the brains."

Images of the night my brother cried because someone told him he had no brains flooded my mind.

Then, *pow*!

I can't say exactly how it all went down, but my arms and legs were whirling about furiously like a crazy windmill on steroids. One minute I was on top getting in my jabs, the next it was Danny on top pounding my face. When we finally broke apart, his nose was bleeding. And me? My eye hurt like crazy and I could barely move my arm.

"That's it for you, you insane idiot. I'll tell you one thing. Andy and me aren't going to shut down the whole talent show. No, just Bennie's act. I can't wait to see your little-whittle brother's face when I tell him how you hated the idea of him being in the talent show so much that you got your friends to help you stop him." Danny picked up his backpack and bike. Andy's eyes were big and shiny like silver spoons. "And just remember, if you have any plans to tell a teacher or the principal, I'm dragging everyone down with me. Especially you, wonder boy." Danny mounted his bike and Andy followed. "See you at school, Wart!" He laughed like it was the funniest thing ever.

After Danny and Andy left, I stood shivering for a long while. For the first time, I understood what it meant to be "between a rock and a hard place," a saying my granddad used. I slowly picked up my bag and winced as I tried to slip the straps over my shoulders. With only one good arm, it was impossible to get the momentum up to actually ride my bike, so I pushed it to school.

No surprise I was late and had to go to the front office to get a late slip. Mrs. Daniels caught sight of me. "Oh dear, you don't look very good, Warren. What happened?"

"Fell off my bike on the way to school," I said, hoping she couldn't tell I was lying.

"Well, you let Miss Charles take a look at that eye of yours," she said.

"No, I'm okay. It's just a —"

"Warren, I insist that she have a look at your eye," Mrs. Daniels said. "I'm going to email your mom as well."

I thought about the dream I'd had the night before of Bennie getting sucked down into a thick, oozing pool of peanut butter with no escape. In that moment I realized the dream wasn't really about

Bennie getting stuck. It was me who was getting sucked deeper and deeper into the muck of countless lies and mistakes.

So now the question was, would it matter if I made one more?

CHAPTER 10

I needed to avoid Maya, the guys, and Bennie all Thursday. During class, I complained that I had a headache and leaned on my cupped hand to hide my black eye. At recess and lunch, I did garbage duty on the far side of the school, away from where the guys were playing hockey, so I could work out the details of my plan to stop Danny. At three o'clock I raced out of the classroom to get my bike. I thought I was home free, but I was wrong.

"Hey, Warren, wait up." It was Maya.

I tried keeping my face turned to the side so she wouldn't see my bruised eye, but it was no use.

She frowned and said, "What's wrong with your eye? It looks really sore. Is that why you've been acting so strange all day?"

I shrugged and said, "It's nothing. I just fell off my bike on the way to school. Hit my eye on something when I fell."

"Good thing you were wearing a helmet," said Maya. She stared at me hard, like she knew there was more than what I was telling her. She was as bad as a second mom.

"Yeah, good thing." I grabbed my bike with my good arm and tried getting on. "Ow!"

"What's the matter? Your arm hurt, too?" asked Maya.

I felt like crying, but refused. "Yeah, it's pretty sore."

"Here, let me help you get on your bike," Maya said. I hated letting her help me, but it was better than walking my bike all the way home. She gave me a push off. Once I was rolling I managed to steer with just my one good arm.

"Thanks, Maya." I had to admit I was glad for her help. But as we rode home, she kept eyeing me.

"Sure is strange the way you fell off your bike and got a black eye. How did it happen?" she said.

"Just not paying attention, I guess." When I tried adjusting my backpack, I nearly lost my balance. "Whoa! See that? Nearly did it again."

Maya wouldn't let it drop. "You know what's weird? Danny came to school this morning with a bloody nose. Did you know that?"

I shrugged. "Nope. Haven't seen him all day. I was on garbage duty at recess and lunchtime. But that is weird. Ha, maybe he fell off his bike, too." I laughed lightly, hoping it would throw her off my track, but I could tell she was still thinking about it, still trying to figure things out. "Hey, just one more day," I said, cheerfully changing the subject. "Tomorrow's Halloween and the talent show. You excited?"

Maya's eyes lit up. "So excited."

After that it was easy. I just let her ramble on for the rest of the ride home by throwing in questions to keep her going.

Mom and Bennie were in the kitchen getting ready to carve pumpkins. "Look, Wart! There's one for you and one for me. C'mon, we can carve 'em together."

"You get started without me, Bennie. There's something I have to do first." I was nervous and hoped there wouldn't be a lot of questions. "Mom, can I talk to you?"

She looked at me, eyes wide. "Warren! Your eye! Mrs. Daniels emailed and said you hurt yourself on the way to school. She said you told her you were all right. But honey, that doesn't look good at all. It's bruised and swollen." She put her arm around my shoulder and squeezed. I winced. "What's the matter? Is your arm sore, too?"

"Yeah, just a little. But I'm fine, Mom. It really doesn't hurt very much." I put on my best smile to get her to stop worrying and then gave her the same story I told Maya.

"I don't care what you say, we should have someone take a look at your eye and your arm," she said, anxiously.

I had too much to do and didn't have time to see a doctor. I did the only thing I could think of. I laughed. "You're hilarious. You're just like one of those overprotective moms you said you never wanted to be — the ones who hover over their kids and freak out about every little cut and boo-boo."

"I am not, and you know it." She frowned. Pretty sure I touched a nerve.

I quickly changed the subject. "Hey, Mom. I have a project for school. I need a few things from around the house. I want to make a poster, too. Is that okay?"

"What do you need?" she asked.

"It's kind of a surprise, so I was hoping you wouldn't ask me about it."

Mom squinted at me, giving me a half smile and a half-worried look. "Warren?"

"It's nothing bad, I promise," I said, hoping she'd let it go at that.

"Oops. Sorry, Mom. I got pumpkin stuff all over the floor. Can you help me?" said Bennie. There was a slimy orange mess of pumpkin guts on the floor and more dripping off his hands, and off the table and the chair, too.

"Oh, Bennie, just wait right there and let me get some paper towel." As Mom dashed to the sink she said, "It's fine, Warren. As long as you clean up after yourself."

I ducked out of the kitchen before she or Bennie could say anything else and spent the rest of the afternoon in my room working on my secret project. After supper I stencilled a witch onto my pumpkin and carved it out. It was hard to say what Bennie had been thinking when he carved his. The best way to describe it was a pumpkin moon full of craters. When I finished, I put candles in both pumpkins and lit them.

"Ah, very nice, boys," Dad said when he came to inspect. "They look particularly spooky." He said the word *spooky* in a silly warbled voice. Bennie bounced around excitedly.

While everyone was in the TV room watching *Monsters, Inc.*, I snuck into the kitchen and gathered what I needed for the next day. I wanted to be quiet and fast so I could get everything before someone came in and started asking questions — and by *someone*, I meant Bennie. Luckily, I was able to fit almost all of it into my backpack. The rest I wrapped in a plastic garbage bag to strap to the back of my bike in the morning.

Just before bedtime, Bennie and I set out our costumes for the next day. Bennie wanted to wear his to bed, but Dad promised he'd wake Bennie early in the morning so he'd have plenty of time to get ready. I knew he would probably have trouble getting to sleep. So would I. But in my case, it was because I wasn't sure what the next day held for Bennie and me, and whether what I was about to do would make things better or worse.

★　★　★

As I headed out the door the next morning, Mom and Dad smiled at me, just as they had every Halloween since I was little. My chin was itchy from the gunk I wore as beard stubble. "Warren, you need to get back in here and shave," kidded Dad. "Oh, wait, you're not Warren, you're a terribly scruffy pirate." He pretended to toot on his hands as if he had a whistle. "All hands on deck and hoist the flag, me mateys. Methinks there's ships to plunder. Arghhh!"

Bennie flapped his arms excitedly. "Aye aye, captain. The pirates are ready!" Half the beard stubble on his chin was already gone. I imagined he'd licked it off along with the peanut butter he'd had for breakfast, some of which was still dripping down his chin. Mom said she'd fix his beard before he got to school, but it wouldn't make much difference since he still had lunch to get through.

My arm was still sore, but I could get on my bike without help. Just before I left, Mom came outside. "Here, take these," she said, handing me a pair of sunglasses.

"What do I need these for?" People had already seen my black eye, so there was no point in covering it up.

"I know you're nervous about the parade, Warren. Whenever I'm a little afraid of something, I wear sunglasses. It gives me a feeling of being anonymous, like I'm incognito or disguised. Try them. They might help." I took them from her and slid them into my pocket.

"You don't think I'm disguised enough?" I said, pointing to my scruffy face and clothes.

She smiled. "You have a point. It's up to you. Maybe you won't need them."

At that moment I wasn't even worried about the parade. What I was really thinking about was whether I had the guts to pull off my big plan. But I would try anything that could help steady my nerves and keep my breakfast down. "Thanks, Mom. I'll see if I need them." I waved goodbye and took off for school.

The school buzzed like a hive that morning. We had Frankensteins and other monsters, a few witches and wizards — including a whole bunch of Harry Potters — a couple of cowboys, and strangely, a whole pile of pirates.

The class was pretty rowdy, and after a while Mrs. Chapman gave up trying to teach and let us play spelling bingo and thumbs-up until lunch. As much as that was a good distraction, I couldn't help watching the clock and fidgeting in my seat. As lunchtime got closer, the muscles in my shoulder wound up tighter and my heart beat furiously in my throat.

"You don't look so good, Warren," said Maya at lunch. "I mean, don't get me wrong, your costume is great. It's just you're looking pretty nervous. If you're worried about the parade, trust me, it'll be over in no time."

Wishing that's all it was, I said, "Sure. Over in no time." Then under my breath I said, "If only that was true."

When the parade finally began, each class took a turn marching around the centre of the courtyard while the rest of the school looked on. The kinder-garteners were first. Some walked with their chests puffed out, happy for the attention, while others spent the entire time looking down at the ground or covering their faces with their hands. Dee Dee Martin cried, but then she was still four.

Finally, Mrs. Chapman was called to lead our class in the parade. The theme song for *The Addams Family* crackled from the loudspeaker. With beads of sweat on my upper lip, I decided to put on the sunglasses and then slid into line behind Maya. She didn't seem to mind the attention of all the other kids watching us parade around. In fact, she was really into it, pointing her wand at the other kids and saying stuff like "Presto, you are now a monster. And

you are Superman. And you are a gingerbread man."
I don't know if it was all the fun Maya was having
or the sunglasses or the scary thing I had to do, but
whichever it was, I wasn't nearly as embarrassed as
I thought I would be. I guess I was saving that for
later. And as it turned out, hiding behind sunglasses
was a good idea. I wondered, though, what would
make Mom feel so nervous that she'd have to hide
behind sunglasses.

After the last class paraded through the courtyard, Mrs. Daniels spoke through a megaphone.
"All right. It's time to make our way to the gymna-
sium for the afternoon talent show. We'll start with
the kindergarteners to grade fours. Then the older
classes will come in."

A lot of the older kids were impatient, telling
the younger ones to hurry up and get seated inside
the gym so we could join them. I looked around to
see where the guys were. I saw David and Jeff whispering about something. They looked a little nervous. I wondered if Danny had told them about his
new plan. I saw Jesse, too. He looked at me with no
expression at all, so there was no way I could tell
what he was thinking. I smiled and gave a little wave,
but he didn't seem to see me.

Finally, our class started down the hall toward
the gym. I thought about Danny's original plan.
It was right there in the hall that we were all supposed to drop our stink bombs. Looking around, I

imagined the chaos it would have caused and snickered nervously at the thought of it.

I spotted Danny up ahead. He was hard to miss since he was a lot taller than the others in his class. He wore a yellow clown mop on his head and his face was painted white, but it wasn't hard to recognize his devious grin as he caught sight of me.

In the gym, I saw there were a couple of rows of parents who had come to watch the talent show. Mom and Dad were beaming and waved at me. That's when I realized how weak my knees felt, and I hoped I wouldn't fall in a heap on the floor.

After we were seated, Mrs. Daniels got up onstage. "All right now, quiet down and we'll get started. First, I want to welcome the parents who have joined us today. Next, I want to remind the students what it means to be a good member of the audience. When a student is performing, you should be respectful, supportive, and quiet. And give a hearty round of applause at the end of each act."

Kids were already getting restless and scooting around on their bums on the gym floor. "We have some wonderful performers for you this afternoon, as well as a couple of surprise acts," said Mrs. Daniels. "I'm sure you'll want to be here to see them. That is, of course, unless you have to leave for poor behaviour." Mrs. Daniels looked right at Riley Bechum, a kid in grade three, when she said that.

The lights in the gym faded. The stage curtains opened to reveal Rosalie Reynolds at her electronic keyboard. Melanie Shaffer was the master of ceremonies and had to introduce all the acts. "Now, ladies and gentlemen, boys and girls, we will begin our talent show with Rosalie, who will be playing 'Ode to Joy' by Beethoven," said Melanie. I didn't know much about playing the piano, but I didn't think Rosalie did, either.

Next up was Kevin Beale, a kid in grade two who played the accordion. It was almost as big as he was, and he needed help getting it on the stage. Mrs. Daniels coughed loudly and pointed her finger at some kids who were snickering a little too much. After Kevin played a polka song, he bowed and we watched him struggle to get his accordion back off the stage.

The talent show continued, first with a bunch of girls doing ballet — boring! Then Simran Agarwal and her friends did an Indian bhangra dance, which was pretty cool. I tried to stay focused on the acts, hoping they would keep me from losing my nerve. But it was all going way too fast and I couldn't ignore that Bennie's turn was getting closer and closer. My hands were sweating and starting to shake. I was afraid that when the time came, I wouldn't be able to make them work properly.

I looked down the list of performers. Coming up was Lyndy on the guitar, then Braden was doing a judo demonstration, and after that was Chelsea doing an origami demonstration. I felt sorry for her, since origami was about as exciting as jigsaw puzzles. After Chelsea it would be Tracy doing another piano song — and then Bennie and Maya.

My feet felt like blocks of concrete and I was sweating buckets when I finally dragged myself over to Mrs. Chapman. "Need to go to the bathroom," I whispered. She nodded quietly, but hardly seemed surprised that I was leaving my seat. As I slipped away, I caught a glimpse of the faces of students watching the talent show. Some looked interested, others were amused, and the rest looked bored enough to fall asleep. I would have been glad if they all really did fall asleep, but I didn't imagine I'd have that kind of luck. Instead of going to the bathroom, I quickly darted backstage, where I'd hidden my pack. I should have known someone would notice me — and, of course, that someone was Bennie.

"Look who it is, Maya!" Bennie hollered. I cringed and shushed him.

"Warren? What are you doing backstage?" asked Maya. Before I could answer, some weird thing behind her caught my eye. It looked like an old photocopier on wheels, with a metal bar covered in wires rising straight up and topped by a computer screen with a mouth and boxy eyes staring at me. The strangest parts were the two arms made of vacuum hoses, each with a baseball glove at the end for a hand. I knew it was a robot, but it wasn't like any robot I'd ever seen — not that I'd seen a lot of robots. What I did know, and right away, was that the kid standing next to it was Owen.

Maya followed my eyes. "Want to meet him?" I nodded. "Hey, Owen, this is Bennie's brother, Warren."

Owen nodded at me and mumbled, "Hi." His eyes were wide and the scar that marked his cheek was bright red. I realized he was probably even more scared than me. I didn't mean to, but he caught me glancing down at his feet.

"You can't tell which one it is when I'm wearing shoes and long pants," he said. "Not until I start to walk."

I felt my cheeks burn. "Sorry, I didn't mean to look."

"That's okay. I knew kids were going to be curious. My parents said I'll get used to it," said Owen. "I hope they're right."

Before I could say anything, Bennie cut in. "Don't worry, Owen. Your robot is going to crush this," he said happily. "Then after that Maya and me are goin' to blow them away with our magic and puzzle. Right, Maya?"

Just then Chelsea ran off the stage crying. As she raced out the door, she ripped up her crushed origami figures and threw the scraps on the floor.

Then we heard Mrs. Daniels speaking sternly. "I'm very disappointed in what just happened, Dylan Munro," she said.

"But it was true, I could see her underwear," said Dylan.

"Dylan, that's enough. Not only was that disrespectful, but it embarrassed Chelsea and made it impossible for her to finish her demonstration. You need to leave the gym and sit outside my office until I come and speak to you." There was some murmuring from the kids as Dylan left the gym. "And as for the rest of you, laughing like that didn't help at all. So you are all guilty of upsetting Chelsea. If we're going to continue with this talent show — and I certainly hope we do, since we have some wonderful performances yet to come — then you all have to do better. Can I count on you?" There was a long pause. "All right, then, let's continue."

The next thing I heard was Melanie's voice. "And now we have Tracy from Mrs. Murray's grade two class playing 'Twinkle, Twinkle, Little Star' — twice."

I felt the blood drain out of my head. "I'm next," I whispered. I felt as if my body wasn't my own anymore. Somehow it automatically walked over to where I'd put my stuff and brought it to the edge of the stage.

Maya looked at me, surprised. "Warren? You're doing an act in the talent show? What? Why didn't —"

I put my finger to my mouth. "Shush, Maya. Not now." Miraculously, she didn't say anything else and neither did Bennie, who actually looked excited.

The next thing I knew there was applause coming from the audience, and Tracy walked off the stage looking very pleased. Then Melanie said, "Thank you, Tracy. That was very nice. As Mrs. Daniels said, we have some surprises for you this afternoon. The first is Warren Osborne, demonstrating a science experiment. I wonder what it could be."

As if I were using the remote control that moved Owen's robot, I managed to command my body to walk onto the stage. The small table I had asked for was waiting there, so I began unpacking my backpack. I was aware the whole school was watching, plus my parents, but I just couldn't look at them. I felt in my pocket for Mom's sunglasses and put them on.

Still feeling like a mindless robot, I said, "Everything you'll need for this science experiment is harmless and can be found in your own kitchen." There was a sudden stir in the gym as I held up my poster. Before I lost my nerve I read out loud the words on it: "HOW TO MAKE A STINK BOMB."

CHAPTER 11

All at once, I heard people gasping and giggling and chattering. Mrs. Daniels rushed over to me looking pretty mad. With her back to the audience she glared at me, and through gritted teeth she said, "What do you think you're doing, young man? When you begged me to do a science experiment for the talent show, I thought you meant something like how to make invisible ink or slime or a volcano. If I'd known you were going to teach the children how to make stink bombs, I never would have allowed it."

I glanced behind Mrs. Daniels and saw loads of kids bouncing happily off the floor. It was the most excited they had looked since the talent show began. I saw my parents, too. Dad's hand was cupped over his mouth, so l couldn't tell if he was laughing or embarrassed or mad. As for Mom, it was easy to tell what she was thinking. Her mouth hung open and her eyes were squeezed shut, which meant she was in a state of shock.

Mrs. Daniels huffed and snorted like a bulldog. She glanced at my parents, then back at me. Finally, she said, "I'm going to let this go for now, but make no mistake, we'll be talking about this later." Then she turned to the audience and said, "We'll go ahead with Mr. Osborne's *experiment*, but only in the interest of science. It is *not* something for you to go home and try. Otherwise I'll be hearing from some very annoyed parents."

When she finally left and I was alone on the stage, I realized I'd forgotten everything I was supposed to say. I searched for the words, but they were gone. I saw my stink bomb lying on the table. I mumbled, "The ingredients for a stink bomb are very simple, really."

"Speak up," someone yelled. "We can't hear you."

My cheeks burned and I tried to clear my throat. "Like I said, making a stink bomb is easy." I held up the bottle of vinegar and jug of milk. "Pour some vinegar and milk into the mixing bowl." Then I held up my eggs. "Next, you will add some eggs. It's okay to use the egg shells, too." As I cracked them open and added them to the mixture, kids were saying "Eww," "Gross," and "Ick."

"If you want to make a stink bomb that's as awful-looking as it is rotten-smelling, there's one other thing you can add." I held up a jar of Bennie's favourite chunky-style peanut butter. The audience groaned in almost perfect unison. From backstage came the word *whee*, or maybe it was *yippee*. Whichever it was, I knew it was Bennie who'd said it.

Mrs. Daniels clapped her hands and waved her arms, but no matter how hard she tried, she could not quiet the kids. They got more and more excited and noisy as I stirred the mixture. But when I held up my baggie with my fully formed stink bomb, they went suddenly quiet.

"Once you've mixed your ingredients well, you can pour the goop into plastic containers or even bags like this one. After that, all you have to do is make sure the ingredients are exposed to a lot of heat. If it's summer, just leave your stink bombs in the sun. But if the weather outside is cool, find a warm place in your house for it to ferment. On a radiator or near the furnace will do. And remember, the longer you leave it, the stinkier it gets." Laughter erupted from the audience like a volcano.

I was relieved my science demonstration was almost over, and at the same time I was glad everyone liked it. Well, everyone except the principal, the teachers, all the kids' parents, and Mom and Dad. But there was still one final thing I had to do, and it was the part that might backfire on me.

I lifted my stink bomb for all to see. "This here is a stink bomb I made many days ago." I heard Mrs.

Daniels gasp. Probably my mom did, too. When the principal started walking toward me, I knew I had to act fast. If only she knew that my stink bomb wasn't the dangerous one. "I couldn't have done this all by myself. It was Danny who came up with this great recipe." The kids began to chatter excitedly and looked over at Danny with admiration. "After the talent show — if you think you're brave enough — anyone who wants to can smell my stink bomb. And I bet Danny wouldn't mind people having a whiff of his, too. Right, Danny?" I nodded in his direction. "And remember, what's Halloween without a little trick to go with your treats?"

"Okay, that's enough, Mr. Osborne!" said Mrs. Daniels.

The kids went rank with excitement, or maybe it was just the boys. For sure, none of the adults looked very happy. I even thought some of the mothers were giving me the evil eye.

Then there was Danny. He gave me one of those if-looks-could-kill glares and mouthed, "This isn't over, Wart!" My heart pounded hard as I imagined all the possible ways he might try to get even with me: pulverizing my face, wedgie pulls for the rest of year, slashing the tires on my bike.

Mrs. Daniels snatched the stink bomb from my hand and said, "I'll just take this for safekeeping. And Danny, I'll take yours, too." He rolled his eyes and pulled from his jacket the same kind of plastic bag as mine, full of chunky brown liquid, and handed it to his teacher.

"Andy's got one, too," I whispered. Mrs. Daniels nodded gratefully.

"Andy, yours too," she said, and waved at his teacher to collect it. I wasn't sure, but I thought he looked relieved instead of mad.

As I packed up my things, the kids applauded like crazy. "Well, you'd better take a bow, Mr. Osborne," said Mrs. Daniels, frowning. "And I'll give these parcels to your parents after the talent show so they can take them home — safely."

I bowed and looked down at my parents. Dad's hand was still over his mouth, but I could tell it was because he was trying to muffle one of his deep belly chuckles. And Mom — well, she was smiling too, sort of, but she shook her head the way she always did when Bennie or I got into mischief.

For now it looked like my plan had worked. I knew I'd pay for it later at a time and place of Danny's choosing, but at least he wouldn't be able to ruin Bennie's act.

When I walked offstage, Bennie ran up and squeezed me like a bear. "That was awesome, Wart. You're the coolest brother in the whole world. How come you didn't tell me you were making stink bombs? I would have helped you. I especially like that you used peanut butter. Betcha it's the smelliest stink bomb ever! Ha!"

"That was pretty funny," said Owen, smiling. "It sure took a lot of guts to pull off a stunt like that in front of the principal and the whole school." It felt good to hear him say that.

Melanie was back on and said, "Now, if you think that was a surprise, wait until you see who we have next. Let's welcome to our stage ... Owen Bradshaw."

Instantly the smile on Owen's face melted away. "This is it," he said. "Wish me luck."

"You don't need it," encouraged Maya. "You're going down in the history of this school."

"Yeah, you'll be great," I said. As Owen limped onto the stage, I was feeling his grief. I didn't know him very well, but at that moment I thought he was the bravest person I had ever met.

But something was wrong. Except for a few teachers and parents, no one clapped.

Why was there an awkward silence as Owen went onstage? After all the applause I got just for making some silly stink bomb, I hated that everyone was so quiet now that it was Owen's turn. I peeked through the side of the curtain to see what was going on. Kids looked up at him, but they appeared uneasy. *Man!* Anything would have been better than that — even if they'd all gone to sleep from boredom.

When I looked to see Danny's expression, he was nowhere in sight. He must have been pretty mad to leave like that. Just then Owen's robot rolled up beside me. It made me jump and then laugh.

"I'd like you all to meet my friend, Reggie," said Owen. Then Reggie rolled onto the stage. And just like Maya said, every kid in the gym seemed to forget all about Owen and his foot. They squealed and cheered as Reggie spun in circles and waved. They got even louder when he began to toss a large whiffle ball from one baseball glove to the other. Owen added another whiffle ball, and Reggie began juggling. That's when the kids rushed the stage to get a closer look at him. And no matter what the teachers said, they couldn't get anyone to sit back down.

"See?" said Maya, who came up beside me. "No one gives a hoot about his foot. Reggie the Robot is going to be the only thing they remember when they think of Owen being in the talent show."

I smiled. "Yup. You were right, Maya."

"And speaking of things everyone will remember about the talent show, that sure was some gag you pulled," she said, grinning. "Wonder what your parents thought about it."

Before I could say anything, a super-loud cheer and applause rose from the gym. Reggie rolled off the stage, followed by Owen who limp-hopped behind him. "So glad that's over," he said, smiling.

"I knew you would be spectacular, Owen," said Maya.

There was a sudden hustle of activity as some kids rolled the audiovisual equipment onto the stage.

Mr. Carlton took his place at the piano, and Chloe went to her drum set at the side of the stage.

"It'll take just a few minutes to set up for our last performance," Melanie said to the audience. "And when we're ready, be prepared for our very own Maya to dazzle you with her magic at centre stage. And behind her, at this very table, Bennie, who I am told is an amazing puzzle maker, will assemble a one-hundred-and-fifty-piece puzzle, one that he's never done before. And he'll do it in less than ten minutes. You'll be able to watch the puzzle take shape on this overhead screen."

Just as I was afraid would happen, there was a wave of unhappy and impatient chatter. Mrs. Daniels put a quick stop to it, though, with one of her wicked stares around the gym.

"And don't forget, after this final act we'll be announcing this year's winner of the talent show," said Melanie. "Our panel of judges is made up of two teachers and two students: Mrs. Archibald, Mr. Li, Jasmine Basak, and Gregory Wilkinson." That brought on some more chatter, but this time it sounded excited.

"Bennie? Where's Bennie?" called Maya. "Oh, there you are. Come on, it's nearly our turn."

It was weird. He'd been talking about this talent show for weeks, but now that it was here, instead of bouncing around and grinning from ear to ear, he was quiet and his face was blank.

"Bennie, where's your puzzle?" asked Maya. "Go get it. We're about to go on." He didn't move.

"Bennie," I said firmly, "get your puzzle."

He ran over and threw his arms around me. "Can't, Wart. It's gone."

"What's gone? Your puzzle?" I looked around. "Where's it supposed to be?"

"Right over there," Bennie said, pointing to a table near the stage exit.

"Maybe it got moved. Let's hurry and look for it," I said.

Maya, Bennie, Owen, and I searched all over the backstage area but couldn't find the puzzle. That's when I got a sickening feeling and ran to the side of the stage and peeked through the curtain. Danny was sitting with his class now and looked to be in a good mood — a very good mood. Fear crept up my spine.

Earlier in the month, if someone had suggested that Bennie's puzzle should mysteriously go missing at the last possible moment, I would have thought it was the perfect plan to keep him from going onstage and embarrassing himself and me. But looking at him now, his head hung sadly, all I wanted was for him to get the chance to show everyone at school what he could do.

I knew this mess was my fault and I needed to fix it, but how? Just then I saw the scraps of ripped-up origami paper Chelsea had thrown on the floor when she ran off the stage. They gave me an idea.

If there was only one thing I knew for sure, it was that Bennie had a mysterious ability to do puzzles. I bet there wasn't a single one in the whole world he couldn't do. And I was going to make sure he got the chance to show his amazing talent.

"Maya, when they introduce your act, you have to go out there and stall for time. I've got an idea," I said.

"What? Are you going to somehow magically produce a puzzle for Bennie?" She shook her head. "Sorry, Bennie. I need to tell Mrs. Daniels that someone stole your puzzle."

"No, don't do that, not yet," I begged. "Give me a chance to figure something out, Maya. Please."

She looked at me hard and long. "Okay. I'll do my best. But you know something, Warren, and afterward you're going to tell me about it!"

I nodded. "I will. I promise." I swung around and grabbed my brother by the shoulders. "Bennie, I need you to go and find a box or a basket — something to hold your new puzzle." His eyes went big and round. "Hurry, we don't have much time. Go!"

I tore out of the gym and headed down the hall. I was looking for a picture of some sort. I didn't know of what exactly, but there had to be one on the walls somewhere that I could use. I came to my classroom and stopped in front of the artwork we'd all made earlier that month. I looked up at my poster. It was something I could use, but not a very good something. Then I looked over at Maya's poster. It was really good — beautiful, in fact — and it had a good message. As I snatched it off the wall and ran back to the gym, I hoped she wouldn't mind what I planned to do with it. When I got there, she had just gone onto the stage. I watched as she nervously cleared her throat.

"Ah, hi, everybody. There's been a slight change of plan." There was a buzz around the gym. "If it's okay, I'm just going to start my magic act and" — she looked backstage and saw me — "and then Bennie will come on … I hope." She smiled weakly.

I turned to Owen. "I need your help. We don't have time to cut this into puzzle shapes. We're just going to have to tear it up into tiny bits the best we can — and fast." Owen didn't look very impressed with my idea. "I know it's kind of lame, but it's better than letting Danny win."

Owen raised his eyebrows at me. "Danny? You think he had something to do with Bennie's missing puzzle? I wouldn't be surprised, but —"

"Never mind about that right now. I just need you to help me, okay?"

He tore off a large chunk of the poster board and began tearing it into small pieces. "Okay," he said, shaking his head, "but Maya's not going to like what we did to her picture!"

I had the same concern, but didn't have time to worry about it. Together we tore Maya's picture until it was unrecognizable. Bennie returned with a shoe-box in his hand.

"That will do," I said. I began filling it with the tiny bits of ripped-up poster board. They were mostly black pieces, but there were some yellow pieces for the moon, and red ones for the lettering. I didn't know how many pieces we'd made, but it was enough to challenge my brother. If anyone else had tried this, it would have been a hopeless cause. But I was confident Bennie could put all those pieces back together so everyone could see that it was Maya's picture.

"Okay, Bennie. This isn't like the puzzles you're used to, but all these pieces go together in the same way and will make a nice picture. So get going. Maya is waiting for you."

Bennie looked at the scraps in the box and frowned. "Wart, you being silly or somethin'? This isn't a puzzle."

"No, I know that, but it's the best we can do right now. Besides, it'll work like a puzzle. A bunch of tiny pieces that fit together to make a picture, right? So go. Everyone is waiting for you to start."

"I can't do it," he whined. He sniffled and wiped his nose on his sleeve.

"Look, do you want to let everyone down? Do you want to disappoint Mom and Dad?" Now I'd done it. He started rubbing away tears from his eyes. "What is it? Are you afraid?" He shook his head. "Well then, what?"

"I told you, Wart. I gotta start with the picture up here." He pointed to his brain. "I gotta have the whole thing in my mind so I know where all them pieces are supposed to go."

I gulped and slapped my forehead. Why hadn't I shown him the picture before I'd torn it all up? Now it was too late. "Ah, Bennie. I'm so stupid. I forgot." If Owen had not been there, I bet I would have cried, too. "I really thought this would work. And to top it all off, I've ruined Maya's nice Halloween picture! She's going to be so mad at me."

"That's Maya's picture? You mean the one with the black tree and birds and all?" Bennie asked.

I looked up at him. His eyes were wide. "Yeah, that one," I said, suddenly hopeful.

"I know Maya's picture. Seen it lots of times in the hallway," Bennie said. "Oh boy, she sure is gonna be mad when she sees this." He shook his head at me.

"Yeah, but Bennie, since you know what the picture is supposed to look like, you could fix it, right? You could take all those bits and put them back together, just like a puzzle. I know you can, Bennie," I pleaded. "And then maybe Maya won't be so mad at me."

He scrunched up his face and looked at the box of paper scraps as if it were a bowl of cabbage salad, his least favourite food. But then he looked at me, the way he did sometimes, and I could feel his thoughts inside me. It was that weird thing that happened between us sometimes — that twin thing, I guess.

"I'll try, Wart. I'll do it for you," he said. Then he took the shoebox and tore off for the stage as fast as his flat feet would carry him. He looked back for just a moment and said, "And you're not stupid, Wart. Not at all."

Maya looked relieved when she saw Bennie. But when he dumped the scraps of paper onto the table, she dropped her magic wand. As she picked it up, she looked back at me as if to say, *And this was your great idea?* I shrugged at her.

Pretty soon kids were whispering and snickering. Fortunately, Mrs. Daniels only had to wag her finger and they quickly stopped. Then she came onstage and said something to Maya. I don't know what it was, but I think Maya told her about Bennie's missing puzzle. I was afraid she might stop the act, but she didn't.

"Um, it seems we have some creative improvising going on here," said Mrs. Daniels. "Should be interesting." Then she left the stage.

Maya turned back to the audience and with a sweep of her wand, she said, "I will now turn this room temperature water into ice — instantly."

I'd seen her practise that trick a dozen times, so I watched Bennie instead. He had already finished sorting the tiny pieces on the table into neat rows.

But instead of beginning to put them together he just stood there staring. I started to freak out, thinking he had lost his nerve or that it was just too hard for him. But a few moments later his hands began whizzing back and forth across the table. Before long he had built the outside of the picture. Then the moon took shape, then the scary tree with all its bare branches and birds. That's when I realized he hadn't been just standing there. He was actually imagining the picture and then studying the pieces to see how they were supposed to fit together.

The kids looked like they were enjoying Maya's magic tricks, but soon they were spending more time looking up at the screen at Bennie's hands turning all those paper scraps into something recognizable. I peeked around the curtain to see my parents. They were sitting up, eyes glued nervously to the screen. Danny was watching carefully, too, only he didn't look so happy anymore.

As Maya finished her last trick, Bennie was working on the words at the bottom of the picture — words he could barely read.

"Come on, Bennie," I whispered. "I know you can do this."

I looked at Owen, who held up his crossed fingers for good luck. It helped knowing he was hoping for Bennie's success, too. When Maya finally turned around to see what Bennie was doing, her eyes popped out. But instead of being mad, she laughed.

Then Mr. Carlton started playing the piano. At first the notes were slow, but the music got faster and faster as the remaining pieces of the puzzle got fewer and fewer. And then the kids started cheering. Some shouted, "Go, Bennie, go!" and others were chanting, "Ben-nie, Ben-nie."

And just like Maya and Bennie had planned, when there were only a few pieces left, Chloe began a drum roll — fast, steady beats on the snare drum. And as the last piece of the puzzle was set in place, she brought her drumsticks crashing down on the cymbals. The explosion of sound filled the gym and brought all the kids to their feet, cheering and clapping. My parents stood up and were cheering and clapping, too.

Funny thing — Bennie hardly noticed all the excitement. He was looking at Maya's picture. It was a little tattered, but still amazing. He had that same look on his face whenever he finished any puzzle. I think it was satisfaction. He pointed to the words at the bottom. "Maya, what's it say?"

She smiled. "It says, 'SOMETIMES LIFE IS SCARY, BUT NEVER LET FEAR HOLD YOU BACK.'"

CHAPTER 12

"It's going to be extremely difficult to pick a winner for this talent show," said Mrs. Daniels. "But our judges will do their best. And while they're deliberating, we have Mr. Carlton's grade seven choir to entertain us." She waved for the choir to come onstage.

Backstage there was a buzz of excitement as we all waited for the judges to announce the winner. I was anxious because there were three people I wanted to win: Bennie, Maya, and Owen.

"Hey, Warren, I hear you like to play hockey," said Owen. Reggie the Robot stood quietly beside him.

"Yeah," I said. "And I hear you're pretty good, too." A flash of sadness darkened his face, and I wanted to kick myself.

"I used to be." A few moments later, he smiled and said, "But I still like things that blow up. How 'bout you?"

"Duh! I love things that blow up," I said.

Owen laughed. "Good. Do you want to come over to my place tonight after trick-or-treating? Your family, too? Dad and I put on a fireworks show every Halloween."

"That would be awesome," I said. I couldn't help being curious. "You're not afraid of fireworks after what happened?"

He looked down at his shoes. "I thought I would be. But my parents — and Maya — helped me get over my fears. Well, I guess it's better to say they're *helping* me. I still have nightmares sometimes, but it's not so bad anymore." Then he broke out into a wide, crooked smile. "Besides, my dad's been working on a totally vamped-up Roman candle I just got to see. That, and I don't want to disappoint the neighbours. The Bradshaw fireworks show is a tradition around here."

Right then I knew he and I were going to be good friends. Maybe even best friends.

When I looked over at Bennie and Maya, who were giving each other high fives, I realized something else. I don't know why it took me so long to figure it out, but from the start, Maya had been a good friend — a best friend, even — to Bennie and me.

Melanie came rushing backstage. "Hey, everybody. You're all supposed to come onto the stage for the announcement of the winner," she said.

All us kids who had been in the talent show filed out to the stage, where Mr. Li was waiting. My parents were beaming, and — no surprise — Mom was still wiping tears from her eyes. I didn't blame her. Bennie did an awesome job. But then I realized she wasn't looking at him. She was looking up at me, and I saw her lips moving. It looked like she said, "I'm so proud of you, Warren."

Mr. Li spoke into the microphone. "Mrs. Daniels was right. It was a very difficult decision for the judges to pick just one winner. We had many exceptional and interesting performances. For this reason, we decided that this year we would have two —"

"Ewwwwww. What's that awful stink?" screeched Melanie. Instantly, other kids were shrieking as something that smelled like garbage, body odour, dog poop, and rotten fish all combined filled the gym. Kids ran every which way until some of the teachers opened the doors to the playground and told them all to go outside.

Mrs. Daniels immediately looked over at me. I threw up my hands. "I didn't do it," I said. Then, pointing to Owen, Bennie, and Maya, I added, "I've got witnesses."

In the crush of kids trying to get outdoors, I noticed Danny. Instead of looking bothered, he appeared pretty cheerful. When I caught up to him, I said, "Where'd you get it?"

He smiled mischievously. "Think about it, Wart. How many stink bombs did we make?"

I chuckled. "Right, I forgot about Jeff's."

"Yup, the last one. Couldn't let it go to waste. Like they say, trick or treat!" He dashed off, but then suddenly turned back. "Hey, don't think I'm not getting you back, 'cause I totally will. But as for Bennie, he did okay. He's a pretty cool dude."

He was right about that. Bennie *was* cool — and he was my brother.

Just then a bunch of kindergarteners dashed past me, squealing like piglets and leaving smelly brown footprints behind them. It was hard holding my nose and laughing at the same time. Even though I knew Mrs. Daniels was going to chew out me and the guys, the look on everyone's face was worth it.

When I finally got outside, I took a deep breath of fresh air. But then Bennie quickly squeezed it out of me when he hugged me from behind.

"Eww, that was so gross, Wart. Was that one of your stink bombs that made the gym smell so bad? 'Cause if it was, it was awesome." He was giggling so hard and being so silly that I fell to my knees laughing.

A few minutes later, my parents found us. "Warren, you are in so much trouble when you get home," said Mom. Then she squeezed me hard and whispered in my ear. "But not until I tell you how proud you made Dad and me feel today. It took a lot of courage for you to go onstage. I don't know exactly why you did it, or why Bennie didn't do his puzzle, but I do know it had something to do with you looking out for him. Thank you, son."

"Mom," Bennie whined. "Can we go home now? I'm hungry."

"Of course. Let's go," she said, ruffling his hair.

"Good. 'Cause ever since Warren showed us how to make stink bombs, I been thinking about having a peanut butter and pickle sandwich."

No big surprise there! We all nearly split our sides after that. When Dad finally caught his breath, he said, "Consider it done, Bennie. You deserve it. In fact, I think we should all have a peanut butter and pickle sandwich."

*   *   *

I've learned it's a problem if you care too much about what other people think about you. I used to be like that, always trying to be someone I thought other people would like or think was cool. But it just made me forget who I was and who mattered most to me.

It was my brother who helped me figure things out. He's the kind of kid who doesn't give a squat about what other people think, but at the same time he has more friends than anyone I know. And he's right — every one of us is like a piece of a puzzle, each one unique, with our own special place where only we can fit. And without every one of us, the picture wouldn't be complete.

AUTHOR'S NOTE

Thank you for reading *The Jigsaw Puzzle King*. I'm grateful more and more people are interested in celebrating humanity's diversity, which includes people of all levels of intellectual capacity. Like Warren learned from Bennie, "Without every one of us, the picture wouldn't be complete."

If you are interested in knowing more about Down syndrome, or about people who have it and are living their lives to the fullest — as my sister, Jane, did — you can find many good library books and websites that offer clear explanations and learning resources. Two good places to start your search are the Canadian Down Syndrome Society (cdss.ca) and the National Down Syndrome Society in the United States (ndss.org).

ACKNOWLEDGEMENTS

A hearty thank you to my writing group — all fine and accomplished writers: Linda DeMeulemeester, Patricia Morrison, Paola Opal, and queen of the comma, Mary Ellen Reid. Your questions and comments helped me to write a better story. I am also grateful for the helpful feedback from Victoria Bartlett, who has been a sounding board since my first book in 2008. I want to express my appreciation to Kathryn Lane for seeing my book's potential. Thank you to Susan Fitzgerald for her sensitive and careful editing, as well to project editor Jenny McWha, art director Laura Boyle, and all the helpful support staff of Dundurn Press. I gratefully acknowledge the support of the Canada Council for the Arts.

Last, but not least, I want to thank my older brothers, Greg and Archie, whose example when I was a teen taught me not to care what other people thought, and my sister, Jane, who had Down syndrome and lived a full and happy life until her passing. She helped me to be a better person and inspired this story.